Love is ~~a~~ Many ~~Splendored~~ things

ALINA LONECK
A COLLECTION OF SHORT STORIES

I dedicate this collection to my two precious adult children, Alex and Natka, and to close friends who bless my life with their presence.
My heart is yours – always.

For small creatures such as we the vastness is bearable only through love.

Carl Sagon

Fiction writing is a strange business [...] You sit down and weave a network of lies to explore deeper truths.

Wally Lamb

CONTENTS

In the Mirror

INTRODUCTION

The short stories in *Love is a many splendored thing* explore bite-size slices of life. Diverse and unpredictable in setting, character and point-of-view, one story does not predict the next nor a beginning, an ending. As the title indicates, love is explored beyond the initial splendour of romantic attachment.

Each of the three sections begins with flash fiction shorts of a few paragraphs and extends into a story from the short's sweet spot of five thousand words. 'Hand in Hand' tells of love in partnership, 'Side by Side', love of one's homeland, family and community and 'In the Mirror', love of self.

The stories in this collection both entertain and educate. Always psychologically astute, they move and amuse, offer insight and hard truths, and are at times, as delightfully over-the-top, as they are, viscerally disturbing.

The ideal reader for this collection is someone who has an enquiring mind, reads to be educated as well as entertained and who wants to discover what lies beneath the surface of situations and relationships.

Story order is arranged with a sensitivity to the reader's emotional journey.

HAND IN HAND

✍ MAL

I'm a man of few well-frozen words and a vast suppository of knowledge. At present I'm in a nursing home 'cos of my weekend immune system – just as well I've made my last will and testicle.

My palate's sensitive. I can't enjoy crabs anymore or any other crushed Asians. Today's dessert was a shocker – chocolate mousse with the texture of topsoil. When my wife inquired, "So what did you have for dessert?", being the pineapple of politeness I am, I replied, "Fertilizer".

She chuckled.

That's what I like about her, she's always been able to see the humus in the terror of my words.

✍ JIM AND BETTY

Jim had needs.

He was beyond middle age, stocky and fit, his hugs virile. His spit-and-polish brown shoes impressed Leah. Such immaculate shoes usually walked major cities, not regional towns.

None of the local women appealed to Jim. A relocated city girl, Leah had declined his too-soon advances.

Damn it! Enough was enough.

Jim had a brainwave. He'd buy a CROW for company. Within minutes he found a site and clicked on, 'Proceed to Checkout'.

He let out a sigh of relief.

Yes. Betty, a Cybernetic Remotely Operated Woman, would fulfil his needs nicely.

⌇ LOVE'S ORB

Rob Weaver was well-hung with ginormous testicles, hence his nickname, Orb. He was a serial monogamist who thrived on one-off sex. He chose only plump relatively young virgins.

To taunts of, "You're too bloody choosy, mate!" he would retort, "Mate, I'm able to be picky in a city where the women outnumber us blokes."

He prided himself as one of the rare twenty percent who'd mastered the knack of insemination while avoiding the collateral damage such promiscuity usually entailed – female sexual cannibalism.

He was one colonial orb-weaving spider who did not think sex was to die for.

⌇ THE REMOVALIST

Jacinta was jealous. So jealous, she decided to remove him, and *that* woman, from her life *forever*. Within six months, she taught herself all she needed to destroy them both beyond suspicion. How dare he and her best friend (both exes now) embrace and claim there was nothing between them. "We've never slept together." Jacinta knew emotional infidelity when she saw it.

Prostrate and immobilised in front of her, she took off his right hand and then his shoulder.

Next, eliminate Sonja. The tool she chose created a continuous cut around her body, and she was *gone*.

Jacinta dragged out her final tool – cut and paste.

Adobe Photoshop.

If only it were this easy in real life.

❧ OH NO, NOT JIM AGAIN ...

Arriving first, and on barbeque duty, Jim noted Leah's new hairdo, grey with a striking silver fringe and bangs.

"Why the new look?"

"I shed my look whenever the fancy takes me. Year of the Snake, you know."

A blank look.

"Thought maybe you'd met a man."

If her eyes hadn't been external, she would have rolled them. "As I've said before, Jim, I do it to please myself."

"Still not looking for anyone then?"

Before responding Leah checked there was no tripping hazard between the barbeque and her chair. "No, not unless the right man happens to land in my lap."

❧ THE LIFE & TIMES OF DAVID

Early adulthood: You're a pro-lifer. Your stunning Australian girlfriend falls pregnant. You map out a beautiful life together. She is silent. The text comes. Abortion. Traumatised, you never speak to her again. *Mid-thirties:* You marry. Ensure it's clear that fatherhood is not part of the pairing. Perfect wife. Perfect life. She desperately wants a baby. Love decrees she stay too long. Divorce. Her clock is silent.

Late forties: Second marriage. Younger wife. Pregnancy. Fantastic parents. Mismatched life partners. Trapped – torment and regret.

You could have had it all.

✍ IT'S ALL IN THE STARS

Wednesday's child is full of woe.

Newspaper Horoscopes for July:

Wednesday, July 4

Zen wisdom applies. Don't be surprised by exaggerated versions of events. Through all the marvellous days and times to come, refuse the delusions of people. Put a firm tug on the emergency brake.

Wednesday, July 11

Challenges at home stem from feeling unappreciated and disrespected. It's time to try something new to break the dynamics and re-educate those surrounding you to be less selfish and more considerate of your needs.

Wednesday, July 18

You'll gain the opportunity to put carefully laid plans in place this week. You need to be ready to adapt to new opportunities as they present themselves.

Wednesday, July 25

You'll gain a sense of belonging that has been lacking. You'll appreciate the chance to connect with like-minded people. A reunion will spawn profound insights and bring you closer together with those you have a fated connection with. If health or intimate relationships are a concern, avoid resuming bad habits you know are counterproductive.

Thursday, August 9 – The Break-up

There is no fragrance to his memory,

only the acrid aroma of ammonia and putrefied promise.

Anomie overlaid by lacquered bonhomie.

A soul uprooted from itself.

A torn page out of a blank notebook.

Tumbleweed looking for fertile soil in others.

Time for me to become Sunday's child – bonny and blithe, and good and gay.

THE SPACE BETWEEN

It was not the words she noticed but the space between them. Voids of glacier white. She'd known a letter would come. Always the circle. The convex cold ferocity of his anger, scorn and loathing. The terminations. Then the concave enfolding tenderness of his remorse. The begging. The promises.

At last, she'd peeled herself away from the licking. Licking his boots. Licking her wounds. Watching him lick his lips. No more salty teardrops mingling with her blood and his spit. This time, triumph and resurrection within her silence – 'perhaps' brought to its knees by a 'never again'.

The rubber stamp with its soft voiceless pad of indigo struck the thin ink onto the envelope. RTS. His rage, torment and spite entombed forever.

Stepping into the sunlight, she let the marital door slam behind her; the letter in her gloved left hand, a green suitcase in the other and, in her pocket, an interstate train ticket to 'Somewhereotherthanhere'.

JUST DESSERTS

Finishing the last spoonful of the tiramisu she let her tongue linger on its liquored creaminess. Licking the spoon as clean as a cat, her thoughts diverted to her ex-boyfriend.

Kidnap him and abandon him in Central Australia with his hands tied behind his back. Add a Bedouin curse, *May the fleas of a thousand camels infest your crotch and may your arms be too short to scratch.* Momentarily distracted, her thoughts quizzed: how many feral camels were there anyway in Australia? She googled. About one million. She added three zeros to the curse of one thousand and felt more ameliorated for the way he had violated her generosity, her hope, her trust and her open acceptance of his inconsistencies and idiosyncrasies. She was an empath, and he had preyed on her forgiving, emotionally sound and romantic nature. Ultimately, what extricated her was that emotional soundness and mental strength.

She'd been patient and observant. Right time, right place. She had certainly never *needed* him for a contented life, although he was always telling her she did. She no longer *wanted* him. He was poison.

Since the early disquieting and incongruent behaviour, what she sought all along was the truth of the situation. For ten months, love and commitment had chloroformed her intuition and pragmatism. She knew what to say to end it. Once freed from contact, she had understood the truth – his actions from the outset were always a means to *his* ends.

She sought now to shed the toxic residue that clung to her psyche like gunk, to transition back into the sunshine letting it percolate through her bathing her skin and suffusing her soul with its yellow life-affirming contented warmth – her spirit sunlit again, her fullness restored.

She'd exhausted herself planting yuccas in her rockery to garden fork depth, so no way was she going to waste her time or energy on digging two graves – his or hers. Six feet under was way beyond her fortitude and willingness.

Neither was she going to submit him to a forced extraction by an avenging duo of ophthalmologist and dentist.

Furthermore, it was winter. A season where no dish is best served cold. It's the season for slow-cooked Persian rice pudding with its sweet fragrant warmth of orange, cinnamon, vanilla bean, cardamom and cloves. Anyway, cold or hot, vengeance is never sweet.

Tit for tat reprisal? *No.* She wanted to keep both her breasts. There'd been enough asymmetrical warfare on his side. Her thoughts diverted again. What is a 'tat' anyway? She didn't care, but she did know it was nonsense along with argy-bargy, hanky-panky, flimflam and hocus-pocus which, by the way, all applied to him.

Decapitate him with a boomerang? The perfect murder weapon. *No!* Bad karma *is* a boomerang. Ultimately, she was substantial enough not to seek revenge. Besides, revenge is an act either of passion or impotence. She felt neither.

Catharsis? Yes. She'd cast him as a character in one of her stories as a cautionary tale to other women. Beware the borderline personality disordered, narcissistic waif.

$\mathcal{8}$ DUMPED

"She's a fucking bitch, Bluey. I want to rip and mangle everything I've ever written for her. Tear it to shreds. Fucking burn it."

"Red, you're going off like a frog in a sock again. I'm too lost, hurt and confused to be aggro like you. Looking at a blank wall day in, day out, I feel used and unused at the same time. Oh, Red … she couldn't get enough of us once. We glided into her life with buttery smoothness, and she loved the intensity of our gel ink. We gave of ourselves freely. Now …"

"Now is shit, Bluey. Forget fucking now. She's dumped us for an upstart from France. Writers are fickle."

"You're not fair to her. We both know why things changed – all those weeks of rain. She needed permanency."

"Grow some balls for fuck's sake, Bluey. Admit it. She's a fickle bitch. Favourites one minute, blown off the next. We're a nuisance to her now. Do you know what *really* pisses me off?"

"I know what you're going to say."

"Damn right, Bluey. Poncy French Bic thinks it's uber-cool. *Euh, ee am so elpful. Ee am so versateel for reh-caw-ding werds.* All those irritating clicks from red to blue, to black to green. Who does it fucking think it is? A member of the Xhosa from South Africa? All show. OMG … serves her frickin right!"

"Why? What's happened?"

"The Bic she's using to edit our conversation has stuffed up. The green is stuck. Believe me, it won't be long before the others malfunction."

"Too true. On the negative side, we are capped and non-retractable but, on the positive, crafted with Japanese precision. Our name says it all. Pen/tel – invented to tell stories. Quick-drying, not instant, was our only flaw."

"I know, I know. You're thinking about the parcels again, aren't you, Bluey?"

Bluey nods as Red continues. "You always want to find reasons to forgive and forget. You've spent too much time on the desk next to the eraser and the white-out."

"*Ha. Ha. Very funny.* When her two adult children moved interstate, she regularly sent small parcels to them. Remember, Red, all those months of rain? She was worried about us; she thought we'd fail her. Sendee and sender blurred into oblivion – undelivered love."

"Oh god, don't get poetic on me. I admit she had a valid reason to discard us, but it doesn't excuse her from choosing to ditch us all together. Where is her loyalty? Her guilt and regret? What about the shared memories? *Ally is an ambitchous wannabee.*"

Silence.

Red recognises Bluey is deep in thought, but he intrudes with, "Oooh, here we go. You're going to get all philosophical on me."

"No. *No.* I'm taking ink from your nib at last. Repeat after me – *we're too fucking hot to be sad or angry.*"

"Good on you, Bluey, that's the go. We're PHAT – Pretty Hot and Tempting. The sooner she bundles us up and puts us in the bag with the things for the op-shop, the better. We'll have our day on the page yet."

𝒟 DIVERGENCE

'*Spl*it' hisses and spits tightly from clenched teeth and an imprisoned tongue, outward, through the slit of taut lips. Its beginning holds the possibility of '*spl*endour', only for such promise to be disdainfully ruptured by its ending.

Ultimately, the choice the three of them faced would be a splendid one or one that would lead to deep fissures. Their brother, Paul, had made his position clear. No matter the outcome, he would be able to look Sylvia in the eye afterwards, and forever. After all, she was a long-term family friend.

Cecilia, the older sister, spoke first. "Dad gave her the money to look after for him. There was never an understanding it was to become hers."

Alice noted the battle cry of her sister within a statement of the known facts.

"True," Alice began calmly, "however, he lent *that* woman he fancied eight thousand dollars and told us not to chase it after he died and we won't. What's another ten thousand dollars?"

Cecilia treated the question as rhetorical. As she looked out beyond her sister to the relentless rain fighting to fracture the windowpane, she pursed her lips and blinked quickly. She wasn't willing to forgo ground to her younger sister in the beginning skirmish.

"That's not the point!"

As Cecilia's voice pricked the air, she rubbed her thumb across the gold band on her left finger that showcased a three-carat solitaire diamond ring whose glittering splendour was imprisoned by the dull day.

"Throw good money after bad? Is that what you're suggesting? There *was no* instruction Dad wished Sylvia to keep it. For all we know, it was set aside to cover funeral expenses."

Alice laughed lightly. "I think that's very unlike Dad. We all know he wasn't a planner. We have Sylvia to thank for him making a will at all."

The air between the sisters was cobwebs and silence. Cecilia's chilly insistence continued. "It's irrelevant. The fact is …"

Alice had stopped listening to her sister. She was acutely aware of Sylvia in the next room and the slightly open doors of the servery hatch. Alice knew Sylvia felt the money was her due. After all, it was she who had enabled their father's wish to remain at home in the final stages of his cancer. She had a soft spot for their father and had offered her time and care with open generosity.

"Look, Cecilia, split three ways it's a relatively small amount of money in the scheme of things. Is keeping it worth the ill-will and resentment it will cause?"

Alice took a deep breath, inflating her chest before delivering the death blow. "If it matters to you, Paul and I will forgo our share, and you can keep yours."

The blank look of defeat shuttered Cecilia's face. A lone villain she was not.

⌁ AN ORDINARY MORNING

By the time she had begun breakfast, clouds had drawn across the sky like an awning dismissing what is preferred, for what is. The breeze bullied fronds and foliage into waves and shivers. Lena poured her tea, a waterfall of warmth and ochre. Outside, the fan on the patio hovered in a three-sixty. Birdsong drifted on the wind from the west carrying within it the essence of life and relaxation. The heartbeat of the clock on her desk anchored both the day and Lena's driftings as she sipped.

Then, smoothness gave way to staccato. The sounds of opening shutting, flushing, opening and slippers on tile. Her daughter was awake. Lena noticed her daughter's hair, fairy floss and knots, but most of all she noticed the smile. It buttered her daughter's face with warmth and promise. Lena knew what would follow. The hug. A hug bears and trees know well.

Breakfast finished, Lena drove beachward as her daughter hibernated bedward.

At the beach the shore was always as it was, sandpaper overlain with pebbles scattered like sequins on the neckline where damp meets dry, the tideline a spilt cappuccino on the beige and dryness. The breeze flirted with Lena's right cheek as it came off the sea, leaving her left cheek virginal. The shrubs along the horizon were drunk and disorderly where they met the sky, *but oh … the sky!* An ethereal landscape of azure and icebergs. Heaven and earth. Heaven on Earth.

⊘ MAMA-GU

Pippin remembers only snatches of her childhood. It is to her, a country road at night revealed intermittently by headlights. Her maternal grandmother, Cissy, or Mama-gu as Pippin called her (Pippin's variation on the South Walian for grandma) lived on the west coast of Britain in what had once been amongst the most famous ports in Christendom. It had sheltered Vikings, launched Tudor warships to Ireland, invited Quaker Nantucket whalers to settle and welcomed Belgian refugees from Ostend. It was, therefore, the appropriate place to appropriate her mother as a two-year-old to be raised by an aunt who was married but childless.

For Pippa and her siblings, Milford Haven was the 'blessed Milford' of Shakespeare's *Cymbeline*. The Wales so happy of family holidays. She's still full of the sensing of those times. Mornings, waking to the *wake-up sleepy head* calls of the gulls within the salt and seaweed breeze as she incubated in a bed of the softest down that cooed, *Stay, the day will wait.*

She remembers the water-heater, a treasure hidden in a corner cupboard in the living room. Oh, the luxury and bliss of fetching a warmed towel, or underwear cosied around it waiting to please. Its lure matched that of freshly baked bread.

Mama-gu was a smoker with empathy for the small. When, as a miscreant three-year-old, Pippin sat under her dining table and destroyed the entire contents of a packet of her smokes, it was she who defended Pippin to her mother and spared her a smacking. She understood that curiosity not malice had lured Pippin and that cunning had placed her under the table. The cigarettes' white cylindrical perfection and their innards of golden aromatic chaff entranced Pippin as had her mastery of their undoing in her cave of invisibility.

Pippin's grandmother was a reserved woman even with her recipes. The secret of her dense dark spicy bread and butter pudding she kept. To Pippin it was an exotic cousin that over-shadowed its anaemic traditional counterpart. It puzzled her as a child why mama-gu would not share her recipe. Pippin did not particularly like it, but she did want to know its dark secrets.

Beyond this, Pippin's memories are scant. She looks for more within a family album. She finds a sepia photo of her grandmother as her mother knew her. As the Welsh say, she was a *merch bert*, a pretty woman, even *merched harod*, beautiful. Her hair is thick, her nose fine, her eyes large. High cheekbones contour her oval face, her gaze is open and warm, yet reserved. The only thinness is in her lips, and yet these add to her beauty, any fuller and they would distract.

In a well-spaced even floral hand with a right slant and long loops to the 'y', the writing on the back of the photo unfurls more of Mama-gu beyond Pippin's meagre remembering.

To my dear, Aunty Eunice and Ivy,

With fondest love from, Cissy.

Pippin's mother had added a footnote:

Darling Mother, how pretty she was.

O THE OUTLIER

Many think without thinking. Such as they believe the poor are passive, insensitive to beauty, indifferent and unreasoning. Drunkards! Dullards!

My father, a wood engraver, was undercut by technology; my mother ran a school from home for the neighbourhood girls. Both were level-headed, vigorous and hard-working, but the trap ensnaring them held fast, and the endless struggle demoralised, exhausted and soured them We always lived (my parents, my brothers, Charles and Arthur, and I) on the ragged edge of poverty in a decaying part of London.

I had a brilliant wayward mind from young. I was irreverent, unorthodox and self-confident. Why is one lauded for following someone else's vision but labelled as wilful for following one's own? Why does it threaten others so? It is a devaluation of self-mastery and personal integrity. I've faced this injustice from boy to old man. Never caring for the opinions of others, combined with my deafness as a result of scarlet fever when young, I felt an outcast. At fifteen at grammar school, I came fifth out of five hundred students. There my education ended. My parents were unable to afford my schooling. It lay to me to take full responsibility for the life I wanted.

I hated school anyway – too constricting for one such as me. As for the size of nature, I knew intuitively there is no absolute scale and that the small are as important, if not more so, than the great. The buried treasures were inside me: creativity, curiosity, idealism, exploration, mental rigour and moral courage.

I learnt many hard lessons along the way. To apply vision and conscience is to be the outcast, be one scientist or artist. Articles I wrote in prestigious journals earnt me less than a hodman. I lived in one place with two worlds, the poor and the wealthy, and each regarded the other as outlandish and had limited understanding of the other. My own world suffered, as it brokered no betrayal of the soul for money or fame, my career exiled to the far fringes of the scientific community. Unafraid, a more significant force governed my life enabling me to accept any hardship that allowed me to be on the move with unfettered freedom to experiment, predict and discover.

Apart from a handful of close friends, even my fellow scientists felt threatened and were dull of understanding. "You know your papers are very difficult to read."

"That may well be," I would reply, "but they were much more difficult to write."

Discoveries were meat, drink and company to me. Through them, I experienced passion, intimacy and commitment – something I would never develop with a woman.

They gave my life meaning and fulfilment much as rearing a family does for others.

Obsessions? I had two. My bike and my housekeeper.

How I loved the steep twisting Devonshire lanes. Anticipation and reaction. Fresh air and nature were respite and restoration for me. Oh, the joy of flying wild and free in the flow of it and at one with myself and my surroundings, disturbing no wildlife or livestock, only the very air itself. The more insanely steep the road, with blasting air on the downhill, the more the madman I became. The thrill of the seamless transition of blinding sunlight to dappled and deep shade as I rode uphill to downhill and from effort to ease. It distressed me greatly if daily cycling was denied me when the weather was inclement or my health ill.

The woman? It was the year 1908, some twelve years after my parents had died, when my sister-in-law's sister, Miss Mary, took me into her home. Middle-aged, she was a virgin as was I. I had incredible intuition for her needs as I did for my work but no formula to be at ease with her or to express my deep affection for her. I was always socially clumsy, lacking tact and the softness of words and touch. I nursed her after her stroke and discovered parsnips cook quickly, carrots do not. Her recovery I attributed to my lack of culinary skills, health her only recourse against the daily blandness of potato and milk soup.

I bossed her around mercilessly. Not intentional cruelty, but a control bred of the anxiety and fear that, without her companionship, I would wither into madness and eccentricity. I am ashamed to say, I forbade her to leave the house without my permission, once taking away her shoes to ensure this. I forced her to wear warm woollen underclothing in winter for fear she would catch a chill. I encouraged her to write to her friends and family but brokered no visiting to the house. I turned her into a shadow of her former self. Eight years later her niece came to take her away fearful for her mental well-being.

As I spent my childhood, I spent my final years. In isolation and with precarious finances. Those such as I will leave a legacy to humankind and in that we must keep faith and be content. My eulogy?

There was a red-haired boy whose father announced, "Do try to be like other people. Don't frown." The boy tried and tried but could not. In consequence, his father beat him with a strap. The boy became an old man with exquisitely manicured nails he painted cherry-red. To bring colour into his grey world soothed and pleasured him.

R.I.P.

Oliver Heaviside

8 May 1850 – 3 Feb 1925

A self-taught electrical engineer, mathematician and physicist who founded cable telegraphy. He predicted and discovered the upper atmosphere (ionosphere) that bounces radio signals back to Earth. It is also known as the Heaviside layer. He believed in the existence of sub-atomic particles and that the mass of an electrical charge increases with its velocity. Although he refused many honours and monetary grants, he was made Fellow of the Royal Society, won the first Faraday Medal and was short-listed for the Nobel Prize. He is the founder of modern-day telecommunications.

⚲ THE MAN IN ROOM 3327

If it weren't for the man in room 3327 the world would be in eerie silence and darkness. Factories would be empty. There would be no radio, no television, no power lines, transformers or electrical substations.

As a child, he is the fourth of five. He is born around midnight. A violent Wednesday night of sudden pelting rain, thrashing winds and pummelling hail lacerating all beneath it. The brilliant bolts of ribboned white-blue flashes of lightning reach earthward from the heavens like the hand of a supernatural creature.

The midwife sees it as a bad omen. "This child will be a child of the storm and of darkness."

"No, he will be a child of the light," his mother proclaims.

Mother's intuition is right. As he grows from boy to man, his ambition is to illuminate the whole world and provide free electricity to all by tapping electrical power from the heavens.

However, at seventeen something hangs like a dark cloud over him.

"You are for the priesthood, Nikola, as I before you and your mother's father before me."

Nine months of hell save Nikola from the priesthood but nearly kill him twice. It commences with hours at a time of vomiting and nausea, followed by dehydration within hours. Exhausted, he lies in his bed sunken-eyed with a thirst he cannot quench as pale milky water, as if rice has been rinsed in it, pours into the bucket placed under him. His skin is dry and shrivelled. His heartbeat falters. Muscle cramps torture him relentlessly. The seizures take him close to a coma. In a limbo between living and dying, Nikola's pain is his father's sermons manifested – the torments of hell and brimstone. It is the evil of cholera. It is both his torture and his deliverance.

"Nikola, you must fight this. If God chooses to save you, I will relent and send you to the best technology university."

Nikola rallies, but survival renders him fastidious about avoiding bacteria. He cannot bear to touch hair. He uses eighteen napkins to clean his crockery and cutlery before a meal. He avoids women with pearls because of the revolting attraction for sebum on the surface and make-up in the silk thread.

The man in 3327 is handsome, slim, tall and debonair and attracts the attention of women, but he never marries. He thinks marriage only for artists and musicians, as they need muses for inspiration. An inventor needs to be alone, solitude births ideas. He cannot name many great inventions that have been made by married men. This knowledge brings him sadness, as he is lonely at times.

He loves the thrill of discovery and creative success but, of all things, he loves books best. He sleeps no more than two hours but dozes to recharge and walks sixteen kilometres a day. He spends hours working in solitude. He is, however, no recluse, as the public and media adore him. In showing his inventions to the public, he is a flamboyant showman – the toast of New York City. High society sees him as distinguished, sincere, modest, refined, generous and forceful. He is a linguist of eight languages and a connoisseur of outstanding food, wine and art. His friends see him as not only scientist and engineer but as poet and philosopher. His secretary sees him as a man with a genial smile and nobility of manner and bearing.

This man is prone to visions where inspiration and solutions come to him after flashes of light. Supernaturally gifted, his memory is eidetic: after brief exposure to images, he remembers them vividly, with high precision and in the minutest detail. Inventions complete themselves in his head without the need for sketches or working drawings. His memory is also photographic; he memorises entire books. Like Einstein, he believes, 'The intuitive mind is a sacred gift, and the rational mind is a faithful servant.' His mind lives in the heavens and the future. He predicts self-driving cars, autopilot and smartphones well before their time.

> When wireless is perfectly applied, the whole earth will be converted into a huge brain, which in fact it is, all things being particles of a real rhythmic whole. We shall be able to communicate with one another instantly irrespective of distance. Not only this, but through telephony we shall see and hear one another so perfectly as though we were face to face despite the intervening distance of thousands of miles, and the instrument through which we shall be able to do this will be amazingly simple compared to our present telephone. A man will be able to carry one in his vest pocket.

He experiences in his later years a soul-crushing all-encompassing love. He is living in New York in a two-roomed suite on the thirty-third floor of The New Yorker Hotel. She is a delicate noble creature, soft-voiced and gentle, and he worships her. He sees her subtle qualities of mind and soul as superior to his.

If she needs him and she is with him, nothing else matters, and there is purpose in his life. If she is ill he nurses her back to health. She is highly social and physically affectionate. They thrive as a pair, and he feels profoundly loved. "I understand her, and she understands me."

One day when she visits him, he knows she is going to die. Light comes from her eyes even more intense than he has ever produced by the most powerful lenses in his lab. As she dies in his arms, something goes out of his life, and he knows his life's work is finished. Until then he was confident he would complete his work no matter how ambitious.

He dies alone soon after her of a broken heart (coronary thrombosis), between the evening of January the fifth and the morning of January the eighth. Ignoring the 'Do Not Disturb' sign placed on his door handle two days earlier, a maid finds his body. It is a cruel irony his passing may not have contained the elegance of the numbers he considered the key to the universe – three, six and nine.

I choose to believe he died on the sixth, the first Wednesday of the year, a windy and frosty day of minus four degrees centigrade with not a storm in sight.

He is eighty-six.

He receives a state funeral.

The female?

A beautiful white pigeon.

Although penniless, found amongst his meagre belongings was a photograph of her, a recipe for birdseed cake and five dollars for birdseed.

The man in room 3327 is …

Nikola Tesla, Serbian American, 1856 – 1943. An inventor, electrical and mechanical engineer, philosopher and futurist. He invented the alternating-current (AC) electrical system that remains the predominant system in use today. He also developed the underlying technology for wireless communication over a long distance.

⌒ THE LAST EGG

Rosie loved to be treated like a lady even though she was an ordinary working girl with two jobs, the second of which she euphemistically referred to as 'pasture improvement'. She and the others lived on a fenceless rural property – nine hundred hectares of flat wind-bashed paddock. Rosie considered roaming freely as food for the soul. She felt sorry for those folks who were confined to living in a space the size of a dining table. A creature of curiosity and habit, she instinctively knew the grass was greener on the other side – the side beyond the unhindered purple thistles. It called to her.

Rosie lived on the property in an old yellow school bus that was moved at night every few days. Each day she woke to the overwhelming noise of the others who frantically flurried off the bus.

A sign on the bus in bold black letters read 'CAUTION', but caution held no value for Rosie, she preferred the wind to claim it. The bus also had a sign 'Licenced to Seat 45 Passengers', but as only she and the others slept in it, all six hundred and fifty-six of them ignored it. Yes, Rosie – a dust-bathing, manure-spreading, high-yield, organic-egg-laying Bonds Black.

As the farm's best layer, Rosie's eggs won gold medals for their great taste. Rosie attributed her success to the fact she'd chosen her nesting place away from the riffraff who nested bum-to-bum three to a box. She preferred to lay in private and selected as her nesting-place a cavity once home to a radiator. To Rosie the conundrum of what came first – the chicken or the egg – was self-evident. First were the hens, then the eggs. Roosters solely inseminated their way into the scenario if more birds, rather than a high-protein breakfast, were required.

Of late Rosie's egg production had dwindled and the shells thinned. She struggled to produce one egg a day. Her nights were restless as she dreamed of yellow fluff and motherhood. Her mornings – the 'egg songs' she sang before, during and after she laid – had lost their sweetness, their cheer, their sound of proud announcement.

Then came the morning of the day she knew would yield her last egg. There was one reason this chicken crossed the paddock –

motherhood and the virile call of Romeo in the lemonwood tree beyond the thistles.

The longest recorded flight for a chicken is thirteen seconds. Like a five-year-old child, Rosie leant forward, head downward and, stamping at full speed, launched herself into the air like an elite athlete. She cleared the thistle patch in nineteen seconds.

Romeo equalled his Shakespearian namesake by choosing Rosie as his one and only. When he'd courted her with his tidbitting, she felt he moved masterfully and called charmingly. She adored the large bright comb on top of his head that offset his pitch-black feathers. She felt secure he would watch over her and provide food. His 'took, took, took' let her know where food was and reassured her ears and her heart.

Life was tranquil away from the three thousand, nine hundred and ninety-nine other chickens. No cramped buses and no wobbling of the landscape with the morning's release. The lack of eddying, swirling, pecking, scratching, clucking and chortling suited Romeo and Rosie splendidly as it did their one-and-only, egg-squisite and egg-ceptional son Chickadee.

7 THE ABBRACCIOS

Number eight was a house that said a white weatherboard hello to two streets. Its rear entrance and garage faced what had been a cattle track but now led tarmacked to a private hospital. Opening on to a perfectly north-facing vista, the front door bathed the living-room with silken sunlight in the mornings. Here is where Anna and Marco lived.

One Friday afternoon in February, the two of them collided on the corner outside their home. Marco was in his overalls as usual, with his toolbox, and Anna had on her favourite white dress with red cherries on it.

Anna noticed Marco's discomfort and he hers. His fingers curled tighter around the handle of the toolbox as her right hand fisted even tighter around whatever she had in her pocket.

"Why are you home at this time? Work slow?"

With gentle accusation in his voice, he replied, "Thought you were home all day!" He put his toolbox on the ground and hugged her. "Aren't you cold?"

She shivered as she always did from his touch. She realised it was four o'clock, and a chill had begun to set in since she'd left in the morning at seven o'clock. The adrenalin from the day was still pumping through her.

Anna had begun the day with five thousand dollars in her pocket and by noon had only eight hundred and sixty-three, with nothing to show for it till the following Monday at four p.m. Online shopping was convenient, but an auction was an event – catalogue, viewing, bidding, collection.

She knew he'd adore what she'd bought him for their anniversary. Under those overalls beat the passionate heart of an aficionado. Although a tradesman of the electrical, he was a man of the mechanical. She knew he'd be all words and hand gestures over the watch's second hand as it glided imperfectly, yet beautifully and calmly, around the antiquated champagne dial and into their future.

Nemos Minimatik Champagner – slender, ideally proportioned and cheerful like Marco. Its neon-orange minute marker hand elegant and a bit cheeky like Anna. Its transparent exhibition-case back, a riot of sunburst décor, tempered blue steel screws and a small constellation of rubies and sapphires. The heart and soul of its workings, a tiny golden balance wheel spinning back and forth regulating time.

The night of their anniversary, he led her to the bedroom. The ceiling was a mesmerising extravaganza of sunbursts reflecting rainbows. A chandelier. She knew straight away, with her heritage, it was Czech crystal hand-poured, hand-cut and hand polished. Rose petals confettied the bed and, softly in the background, she heard their favourite romantic aria, 'Nessun Dorma' from Puccini's *Turandot*.

Anna and Marco had been childhood sweethearts. When he first met her, he knew she was the one he would marry. She was fifteen and he was twenty. Anna took time to win over, but here they were on their fifteenth wedding anniversary enveloped by light and time united in the knowledge that, at the right time, in the right light, everything is extraordinary.

THE WRONG MAN

Relationships end for a single reason. Infidelity. Abuse. Incompatibility. No explanation needed. But sometimes, a reason requires a story. This is such a story.

Summer

Samantha Bonner believes in making her own sunshine, preferably shaken and stirred by a warm breeze and saltwater. She dives into the limpid ocean and, as her body glides across its infinite crispness, she notices the surface undulations diamond-studded in the sunlight and the sandy-slivered fingerlings that dart beneath and across her path. This is Heaven on Earth. Exiting the water she lets out a soft, "Oooh, so nice." She suns herself dry. Lying there, the need she's felt for months rises in her breast subtle and instinctual – longing and desire. She doesn't want her bare imprints on the tideline's wet sand to be forever those of a solitary in thought. She wants footprints of paired chatter: size elevens alongside her sixes. Her right hand stirs the depths of her beach bag. Found it. Her index finger taps the phone icon on her iPhone.

"Hello, my darling friend, guess what?"

"Hi, Sami, you sound excited. I'm taking a punt that whatever the guess what is, it's good news."

"I've decided to do what you've been telling me to do for ages. I'm going online to look for a good man to share my retirement with."

"That's fantastic. I'm so pleased. You've got a lot to offer. You're attractive, smart, loving and loyal, with the patience and wisdom of a saint."

"Thanks, Jenna … ooh, hang on a minute … I think I've just developed swelling on the brain, and my halo needs an upgrade."

"Ha-ha. You're a hoot."

"I'm thinking about RSVP. Madeline's niece is married to a great guy she met on there. Her family adores him … mind you … Madeline didn't do so well."

"Look, sweetheart, it's a mixed bag out there. You'll be fine. Keep me posted."

"Will do. I love you. Bye."

"I love you too. Good luck."

That evening Samantha logs into RSVP and, confident Van Morrison won't mind, decides on 'Tupelo Honey' as her profile name. She types: *My photos are from this year and untouched by the edit button; although, at my stage in life, I present better by candlelight and minus prescription glasses.* Why do most men think women lie about their age? She'd never do that. Tell one lie and all your truth becomes questionable. Next question. What are you looking for in a man? She wants to avoid it sounding like a shopping list, but she knows what she appreciates: kindness, intelligence, wit, humour and fidelity. What's important to her in a partner is a man with a stable, robust sense of self, connected to others and contributing positively to their lives.

Account activated. *Phew!*

During the first three weeks, her RSVP inbox is a steady stream of notifications. Online texts, phone calls and then coffee – rounds of one or two-way eliminations. Third up is Martin. He drives an hour and a half to meet her at Anchor's Wharf Restaurant for lunch. *Three brownie points.* He's well educated, and the conversation flows. *Two brownie points.* Sometimes his questions are too probing – *minus two.* He insists on paying for lunch. *Plus two.* It's a relief he's not a there's a moth-in-my-wallet sort of a guy. You know, the ones who ensure they don't pay the extra fifty cents because 'hers was the soy cappuccino'. She's met a few of those. When she and Martin leave, he opens the door for her, and then asks, "Well, would you like to catch up again?"

"That would be great. We'll chat during the week." She goes to hug him. He kisses her full on the lips – *minus five.*

A stream of unsuitable others follow on from Martin, including those who have played the online game too long and can't be bothered to make any effort. "I'll be passing through Grafton on the way to a fishing trip. I could meet you at McDonald's for a coffee."

Seriously? Seventy-nine kilometres for a substandard coffee?

After the first three weeks, the messages slow to a trickle. Samantha's fended off the odd-bods, the twenty-five-year-olds and the over-sharers. *Really*, does she need to know the reason a man stayed with his alcoholic wife was that she was intelligent and the sex was fantastic?

Samantha is over it all by the time she agrees to a walk on the beach with Mark Hollerman – Karm47. She's impressed by his inventive letter-play. He appears charming, attentive, authentic, well-travelled and intelligent, *and* he drives for Meals on Wheels twice a week. His teeth distract her; they look as if they've been laid by a tiler. Hollywood has a lot to answer for. She thinks of her overbite; at least her teeth are naturally straight. She shares her travel to-dos. "I'd love to visit Japan and then, from Vladivostok, take the Trans-Siberian into Russia and finish in Poland."

"That's amazing. All those places are on my list too."

Mark's response surprises Samantha: raised eyebrows, open mouth and upward-facing palms. He must *really* want to do that. When their walk comes to an end, he asks, "Would you like to see a show next week at the club? I'll pick up the tickets."

"I love live shows. That'd be wonderful, Mark. Thank you."

The night of the concert, Mark picks her up. Samantha opens the door in a black off-the-shoulder, below-the-knee sheath dress with three-quarter sleeves. She's accessorised entirely in white. "Wow!" is all he says, but she sees the hallelujah in his eyes, hears it in the tone of his voice. She glances at his navy tailored jacket paired with café au lait trousers and spit-and-polish Oxfords. Clothes always look good on tall, lean men. "You look so debonair. We both brush up rather well, don't we?"

At the end of the evening, when he says goodnight on her porch, he cups her hands in his. "You must have sensed how hard it was for me to keep my eyes and hands off you. Your long neck. Those beautiful shoulders."

"Perhaps," she says, but really she had no idea. He kisses her on the cheek, and she relaxes into knowing Mark is a gentleman and that she wants to explore a relationship with him.

So much they do together is a perfect fit. Cooking together, Mark and Samantha's tempos are in unison; he finishes chopping just as she's ready to cook. At rock'n'roll lessons his lead is firm but gentle. Apart from one another their texts are frequent, flirty and loving and their phone calls long.

Two months into the relationship, he arrives at her house and greets her with, "You know, I was listening to a podcast and this writer … I can't remember her name … was saying that the best way to describe herself was that she was a sponge always soaking up ideas, and I thought, *that's you*. Now I understand why, when we go anywhere, you read every informative plaque and google every passing fancy. You *really* are so *delightfully* and *uniquely* you."

Oh my god! Mark sees her, he understands her, he knows who she is. "This is the first time in a relationship I've felt truly seen for who I am."

He holds her close.

He feels like home to her.

Autumn

Mark potters in the garden the mornings he sleeps over. Hearing him whistle among the greenery makes Samantha's entire body Frangelico-infused. Is she in love? Not yet. Smitten. That's the word she'd use.

One morning, three months into the relationship, there's an, "I love you, Sami. It'd be great if we lived together." She's taken aback. Partnership, home and belonging. She gets it. He has none of the three. It must be unsettling at seventy to be living in a caravan no matter how well set up it is. "Mark, it's wonderful to hear those words, but I can't reciprocate. It's just too early for me. I so enjoy being with you, but we still don't fully know one another. You haven't seen me stressed, irritable or revoltingly sick. Could we take a step back for the moment?"

Days later, there's an, "I adore you, Samantha."

"What do you adore about me, Mark?" He's silent. There's a nonplussed look on his face as if he's been asked a question he can't answer.

In the weeks that follow, Samantha notices other incongruent behaviours she struggles to understand. He's taking over in the garden. One morning she pops out for his favourite newspaper, *The Weekend Australian*, and returns to find he's removed a small glossy-leafed tree she rather liked. "It had to go. It blocked the view of the pond from the patio." She wishes he'd checked all angles. The bedroom is now without privacy.

The pruning continues the weekends he stays over. He confiscates shrubs and small trees without consultation. Samantha tries to get her point across light-heartedly with a hug and a smile. Smiles always reassure him. "Mark, I truly appreciate all you do in the garden. I love the lumberjack in you, but the garden's becoming a *Where's that shrub gone?* Thank goodness neither of us owns a chainsaw. Remind me to keep you well away from aisle twenty-two at Bunnings." He stares at her and says nothing. The two-way channel's on mute. She's become a soliloquy mired in sludge. He returns to the garden and downscales the pruning to excess offshoots from the golden palms. Samantha smiles to herself – boys and sticks, men and lumber.

A few weeks later, there's another garden incident. Samantha does not want to look out on piles of garden waste and worries about vermin and snakes. She begins to remove one of them.

"Leave it!"

It spits out from between his lips like charcoaled bread from a toaster. It's a stalemate. She removes the piles when he's not there. Of course, he'll notice. He'll say nothing.

As autumn increasingly loses heat, and leaves rust and fall away, the air between Samantha and Mark becomes laden with the covert – his withdrawal, his withholding, his stonewalling. Everything in the garden is *not* fine.

Marina Prior and David Hobson are on tour with their *The 2 of Us* show and are appearing at the local RSL. Samantha's keen to see them. "I think we should go. They're both legends of opera and musical theatre: *Les Misérables*, *West Side Story*, *La Bohème*."

He is non-committal, so Samantha arranges tickets with her I-love-a-live-show girlfriend Michelle. A girls' night out.

A few days later at Tuesday night's rock'n'roll class at the RSL, Samantha nips to the loo before they head home. She meets him in the foyer, but it's not till they are at home he tells her he has bought a ticket to the show. She's astounded, but then again he does have a habit of uncommunicated three-sixties.

"I wonder if your seat is anywhere near us, Mark?" She unpins the tickets for Michelle and herself from the memo board in her walk-in pantry. "Fifty-eight and fifty-nine."

He's incredulous. "Mine's sixty. What are the chances of that, Samantha? Same table and a seat near yours. What a coincidence."

"Wow! Unbelievable. *"*

Something deliberate, slow and precise is playing out. So imperceptible at first, Samantha becomes a player in it, but the script and the part she plays are withheld from her. He's sucking the vitality out of her with his constant need for validation and compliance. Weekends together – cottonwool and eggshells. She's becoming someone she struggles to recognise, a lit candle in a draughty corner. She doesn't understand why, after six months, after she's fallen in love with him, sex has become as infrequent as their shared outdoor activities. It's as if Mark is going through the motions, as if acting a part is catching up with him. She's beginning to see he uses sex and certain behaviours to control her when he feels insecure. What was once cute banter morphs into the monotone violence of barbs. Samantha no longer feels safe, seen, heard or held. Forgetful now of the small things, one morning she asks him, "What time do we go to singing tonight?"

"What time do you think we usually go?"

"I'm not sure, that's why I'm asking you."

A raised eyebrow, an impatient breath. "You know you don't remember things that clearly. You probably don't even know what the date is today."

His response unsettles her.

Myriad indirect hints about moving in lurk, but Samantha is not accepting responsibility for housing him. It is his problem to solve, not hers.

"My son wants to borrow the Kedron Top Ender in April to show his American girlfriend around Australia."

"Where will you live if you agree to that?"

"It's going to be cold in the caravan over winter."

Samantha ignores the statement.

"It's damn difficult keeping track of things when they're in three places: my caravan, the storage shed and your house."

"Mark, you really should rent somewhere of your own. We've talked about this before. It would make things so much easier for you." It would also prove something of paramount importance to her – is Mark with her solely because of her home? She knows he won't rent. Since the concert his wallet has been a thin sandwich in want of her filling. She's been more than fair. Five months after meeting him, she had to stay in Sydney for a week for eye surgery. She was relieved he was happy to come with her and drive her back in her car. Samantha made it clear she'd pay for petrol, accommodation and any associated costs. It dismayed her that the only time he reached into his wallet was for a serving of fish and chips at the beach on the last day. It was worse than the time he'd bought an eight-dollar sandwich to share and asked her for half the cost, especially after all those three-course meals she'd cooked him.

Meanness, so unattractive.

Still, there are worse things a man can be.

One afternoon the week before their planned trip to Vietnam, out of the blue comes, "I don't think being faithful is that important. My mother and father had affairs. They stayed together and became closer as they got older."

What! They'd discussed the importance of monogamy from the beginning. Had Mark forgotten her profile? What had happened to his mantra, 'Trust and Be True'? It's shifting sand too far. She knows the dangers of quicksand sand; she's read *The Worst-Case Scenario Survival Handbook* and noted its sub-title *Great Escapes and Entrances*: toss what's weighing you down; take a step or two backwards; pull yourself out with whatever is at hand. If all fails, float. She takes a deep breath, then slowly and deliberately says, "Mark, it's over." He takes a step back, sucks in his breath, says nothing and leaves. When the front door closes, Samantha lets the air escape deep from within her lungs, long and slow. It's a breath she's held for far too long.

What to do? Return flights for two have been booked and paid for but not the hotels. Damn it, she's going anyway. Mark can do what he sees fit. He pulls out. For the first time in eight months, she feels she can breathe.

At midnight the day before departure, her phone pings with a text message alert.

I've decided to go. I've booked a hotel in Hanoi for sixteen days.

What! He hates cities; there's a whole country to see. She texts back.

You must be mad or drunk.

She understands Mark deciding to go but, Hanoi, for sixteen days? This man has no sense of who he is. His responses are either set in stone or cartwheel and flutter adrift on an anxious, shifting breeze.

There's a text from him the morning of their late afternoon departure.

Can I get a lift with you to the airport?

She's not sure if he's still wanting things from her or is just too mean to pay for a taxi. Probably both. Samantha doesn't want to be petty. She responds with, *OK.*

Sitting next to him on the plane, she's surprised by her composure. Whatever they had is in the past now. She's never been a waverer; she is travelling alone when she's there. A song from the musical *South Pacific* starts up in her head. 'I'm gonna wash that man right outa my hair and send him on his way. Yea, sister!' Oh, that's comforting – like a pacifier to a baby.

"You can stay at my hotel in Hanoi if you like," he says casually. "It's a double room."

"No need. I've booked a room in the InterContinental Westlake."

During the three weeks, she travels solo happily and enjoys the pure luxury of hotels with pools – a blissful swim before breakfast and at the end of the day. In Hoi An she hires a local moto driver, Chum, and explores with the sun on her skin, the wind in her hair. She is fulfilled. She is free. She ignores Mark's texts – his problems are no longer hers.

On the one a.m. return flight he has the window seat. He lifts his right arm. "Come here, rest against me, it'll be easier to sleep."

"Are you sure? You look very cramped."

"I'm fine. Really."

She leans back against his chest, her head on his shoulder. He strokes her hair tenderly. She is not fully aware it is all a deliberate technique to lure her back.

They reunite on their return.

Winter

Samantha refuses to respond to Mark's continuing hints about moving in. Sensing his mounting frustration, she's surprised when he suggests a fossicking trip to Tingha in the Kedron Top Ender. The caravan is like the playhouse she had when she was a child – intimate and compactly perfect.

On the way they stop overnight at Native Dog Campground in Cathedral Rock National Park, Ebor. The star-luminous sky is clear and moonless as the crackle and blaze of a massive log fire warms their fronts as their backs chill in equal measure. Mark connects the BOSE to his iPhone playlist, and opera overwhelms the icy darkness.

Struck by the beauty of it, Samantha cries. He looks at her with moist eyes and cradles her.

This trip however, is when Mark Hollerman shape-shifts to Mark Pettiman. Mark Pettiman, the man who deliberately and unintentionally didn't fill up the water tank in the Kedron before they left. The man who stores plastic buckets and caravan paraphernalia in the shower forcing Samantha to say, "I need to have a quick shower. You know I'm in there for under ten seconds. I need to freshen up down under." She feels a little humiliated having to spell out her hygiene needs. He hides the hot water bottle under the bed so she can't use it. He buys two-dollar white bread knowing she only eats sourdough. She challenges him, he relents. It becomes the pattern of the trip.

The day before heading back home from Tingha, Mark decides to do some sunrise fossicking. "I'll be back for lunch." At midday, Samantha begins to prepare lunch. One o'clock ... two o'clock ... no show. Mark has the car, the caravan park no bikes, and she hurt her toe when she walked barefoot into a wall at home in the dark the day before they left. She's stranded with no good book to read. By late afternoon she gingerly makes her way to the town's cemetery. There, she uprights what yesterday's wind blew over and scattered, and she leaves the cemetery feeling less like a stranger in this township of boulders. Mark returns at dusk – no explanation, no apologies. He doesn't want her to help him with the dinner. He sleeps with his back to her. They're a pair of strangers in tinned cold storage.

Progressively and inwardly, Samantha becomes the husk of a cicada shedding, her inner happiness and confidence browned and brittle – her lover is now her adversary. Time is consumed managing his feelings and unspoken demands, leaving no time to build a relationship. Her body's adrenals pump cortisol and inflammatory chemicals; long gone are the days of dopamine and serotonin as chi drains from her like a tap in need of a washer. Mark's dissonance has done this to her, and she, she has allowed it in the belief that relationships take work but suspecting it shouldn't be this hard.

The evening of the fundraiser for ovarian cancer is the night Mark Hollerman reveals the second man lurking inside him – Phil Anderer – when he makes a deliberate choice to sit apart from Samantha to send a message to the woman across from them of his sexual interest. Samantha is hurt and incensed by his eyebrow-flashing and man-on-offer crotch display.

What's evident to Samantha is apparent to the others close by who glance over, look away, mutter and nod among themselves; he needs to revive himself with another woman with sleek dark hair, a kitten-nose, anaphylactic lips and breasts that would be more at home on a soccer field.

His two-way conversation is all chilli and hot chocolate, *we* and *us* inconsequential and forgotten. *How dare he behave like this!* Worse is coming. Samantha's jaw tightens vice-like, and hot ice rises in her chest. She's distracted for a moment, as a friend taps her on the shoulder to say goodbye. As Samantha turns back, she hears the faint but characteristic click of a retractable pen, glimpses a beer mat deposited into a handbag, witnesses Phil Anderer's right hand slide out across the left side of his chest between jacket lapel and shirt. It's the crossing of the line – the line between sexual attraction and intentional infidelity.

When Mark and Samantha leave, twilight has turned to dank dusk. They walk the fifteen minutes home in severed silence. He hasn't proffered his hand for her to take as he usually would. He isn't walking kerbside either. She hunches her shoulders and tucks her hands under her armpits against the callous chill of the night, her head a hot confusion of thoughts, her heart stuck on pause. She knows when they reach home there will be a third aberration. He will walk through the door ahead of her and, when he does, she knows what she must do: hold onto her values, be true to who she is and abandon what places her at risk of compromising both.

Mark takes off his shoes, plonks down on the lounge in the media room and reaches for the remote. Samantha tentatively follows him in. The timing's not right for an 'I-need-to-talk-to-you' conversation, but she's now a car with its brake-line cut. "There's something I need to ask you."

He looks at her like she's a piece of grit in his shoe. He says nothing.

She sits down on the couch as far away from him as possible, asks a matter-of-fact question in need of the staccato simplicity of a yes or no. She is attentive to timing and clusters that will tell her the one thing she needs to know – will he lie to her? Within the first five seconds, she asks him three times, "Did you arrange to catch up with that woman?"

The living room swallows the silence; it settles in the corners numb and skeletal. He's a marble statue on display whose blank eyes pin Samantha like an overturned truck. The prolonged eye contact tells her one thing. He is not a deer in the headlights, he's a compulsive liar put on the spot. *Failure to answer – liar.*

Behind his frozen façade his mind is thinking at a thousand words a minute; he is buying time to decide how to respond. He cannot admit a 'yes' because everything will crumble within him and around him. Samantha's learnt that shame for him is nothing more than the discomfort of being unmasked. She asks a fourth time, "Well, did you?" She waits for the first trickle and the stream of deviations that will follow.

"People chat. Some – people – happen – to – be – women."

Does he think she's stupid? *Failure to deny – liar, liar.*

She is silent. She knows what she saw. She now knows Mark.

He rises from the lounge and circles around to the right of her like a hyena about to scavenge on leftovers. Samantha waits … still no yes or no. Shock? Hurt? Indignance? There is none of that.

"You're so damn distrusting and insecure. Have you been burnt before?"

Enough already! She has known for some time the nine words necessary to sever the relationship. Out they spill. "I've decided I don't want to live with you."

All he asks is, "You mean you never want to live with anyone or just not with me?"

She is in no mood to be generous, to share any more of herself with him or let any of her energy flow into him. Armoured, she is calm and forthright. "It's a decision I'm making at this moment in time and, at this moment in time, you are the person I'm making it about." It's so icily perfect. She's stunned and appalled when he asks if he can take home some of the dessert she made, and promised him, the previous night. She wishes she was the sort of woman that would tell him to *fuck off*.

Within the week he comes twice to remove his belongings stored in the garage. He'll have to go back to paying a hundred and twenty-five dollars a month for a storage shed. When he returns for the last time, Samantha has already filled the empty spaces left by the absence of his belongings.

"You've wasted no time in rearranging things." There is no hurt in his voice, only accusation.

"I did that because I couldn't bear to look at the empty spaces." He says nothing.

Samantha knows he does not believe her words. He can't trust her truth because he can't trust his own. She avoids looking at him. Finished, he stands in the driveway with the detached amusement of someone who is playing a game. A burning sensation rises into her chest and throat, souring her mouth. Ashamed she ever loved *this* man, she turns her back and presses the garage door controller on the wall.

The roller door wheezes and clanks until it hits concrete.

Spring

Extricated, Samantha's left with a toxic residue. A black sticky soot clings to her psyche. She rebukes herself with *I ought to have, I should have;* yet, she was so close to mental collapse she struggled to think clearly. What most does her head in is trying to determine what was real and what from the outset was a crafted illusion. It takes Samantha a month to realise she's unable to process and heal the damage the relationship has caused. She needs professional help.

Samantha is grateful that the Women's Resource Centre will see her immediately.

The counsellor Emily understands the dynamic completely: borderline personality disorder. He's a narcissistic waif. "These types of men are involved in domestic violence: emotional, physical, psychological. They look for women who are empathetic, generous, compassionate, tolerant, loyal and forgiving. They also look for a strong woman but resent her strength. Strength is a threat."

"I'm a wise, intelligent woman. Why did I not figure this out sooner?"

"Think of these people as a black hole, a parasite, a vampire, an abyss that can't be filled. They're masters at sourcing a supply of energy, adoration and, in some cases, money. Take away their supply and they have nothing to offer. I had a client recently who'd been married to one for forty years. Only now is she realising what she was dealing with all those years."

"Really ... poor woman. I know I felt like I was going crazy."

"Women trapped in relationships like this often suffer from deep depression caused by years of criticism and contempt. When the abusive spouse dies, the partner is conflicted between grief and relief."

"What makes those with BDP like that?"

"People with borderline personality disorder have problems relating to themselves and others. They don't know who they are, which is why their behaviour is so inconsistent. They lie and can't admit mistakes because they already feel less-than. They avoid feeling shame at all costs."

"Will he do this to someone else?"

"Absolutely. Your ex will feel no remorse and have no desire to change. BPD's often suffer from anxiety due to a deep sense of emptiness and isolation. That's why, even when it's over, they hover even though the woman's made it clear she wants no contact."

"*Oh my god*, that's what he did with me. I made it very clear it was over. No contact. But he just kept on going – a blaming petty letter in my mailbox, texts, emails. I blocked him. Relentless, he'd pop up in my mailbox with *yet another* email address. I felt like a mouse being toyed with by a cat. I called the police, and they rang him. Apart from one last text – *May your god forgive you* – he's left me alone."

"Are either of you religious?"

"No … just a barb to make me feel bad about myself."

"Calling the police was a smart move. As you discovered, once outed, they stop hovering. Otherwise, it's another week, another month, another year."

The session time is up.

"Thank you so much, Emily, for tiding me over till my first appointment with the psychologist. I was desperate to have my experience validated. Most of my friends simply didn't understand. I'd share things, and they'd look at me strangely as if I was making it up or exaggerating. Only one of my closest friends, Jenna, understood because her ex-husband was cruel and controlling."

With the relationship behind her, everything is see-through to Samantha: what confused her, what she didn't see. She begins to see the bitter demise of Mark's marriage in another light and why his ex-wife hired a top solicitor and told their only son (who was thirty-two at the time) never to mention his name again in her presence. Samantha understands why, after a long, stressful marriage and at least two affairs – well, the two he had chosen to share with her

– his wife blamed him for her ovarian cancer. At the time Samantha spouted something from a podcast – men have affairs to stay in a marriage, women to leave it. She can see him now. How her words lapped gently over him, suffusing his eyes with a preferred reality; the persona non grata now believed he was the long-suffering, worthy hero. His response to her tears in Ebor? She was just a mirror in which he saw himself reflected. Her confusion over his behaviour on the Tingha trip? He resented her being in his home. Everything made sense. *What an idiot she'd been.*

After eight monthly sessions with the psychologist, Samantha is a woman laundered.

She's regained much of who she is but, beneath the surface, she knows she will never be the same – something lost, something gained. She'd valued him, loved him, and that was her undoing. He'd lured her with her wounding: to love and to be fully seen and loved in return. Eventually, she had challenged his truth, and he'd shrivelled like thin plastic before a flame.

Samantha Bonner is sure of one thing – she will never, never, never kiss beneath a parasitic plant again. With her newfound awareness, she lets go of one female friend of a few months with similar traits. In quick succession, life tests her with Lionel and Robert, newcomers to her informal social circle. She susses Lionel out in a few weeks: an attention-seeking, immature wuss. Gone. Robert? She doesn't even go there.

What she is not sure of is how deeply the collateral damage has wounded her. Currently, the red hand on her compass is facing towards the safety of the solo and the celibate. Samantha's no feminist, but perhaps Gloria Steinem was right: *A woman without a man is like a fish without a bicycle.* But then again, summer is just around the corner.

SIDE BY SIDE

⟡ BLACK AND WHITE

Change for Simon was not an accumulation of moments. It was singular. His office patched through a call to his mobile in Accra. A high-profile client about to fly from Tokyo to the US on a private plane.

"Simon, I'm pissed off. Your office in Tokyo has not put my favourite PlayStation game on the plane."

Silence.

"You should know, Simon, my life isn't meant to be this difficult."

Simon cast his eyes across the African e-waste dump – toxic fumes, burning waste and the open sores on the child scavengers. Without dropping his gaze, his forefinger tapped the red circle on the screen of his iPhone.

⟡ LITTLE DORRIT

Roses scented his hotel room, a reminder of New Year's Eve. Michael had been on the beach with friends – a three a.m. inebriate.

She was there, a girl about six, tired and hungry. They offered her food, but she was too exhausted. She had five long-stemmed red roses. One dollar each.

Michael turned to one of his friends who spoke Cambodian. "Ask her why she doesn't go home."

"She can't until he has sold them all, or her mother will be angry."

Michael knew then that the distance between abundance and impoverishment is a nine-hour flight.

 A SNAPSHOT OF SMALL

"What's that?"

"What's what?" Alex deflected, embarrassed by Bentley's loud voice and pointing. Alex was also unsure how to explain 'short of stature' to a four-year-old whose only frame of reference was *Willy Wonka and the Chocolate Factory*.

Bentley shifted focus. "Why does he need a phone? He's so small."

"To call people, Bentley."

"But he can't pay for anything."

"What makes you say that?"

"Because he's so small."

The man disappeared. Relief. Alex popped some liquorice into his mouth.

"Can I have some?"

"You don't like liquorice, Bentley."

"*Yes, I do.*"

Alex gave in as they were a near a rubbish bin, and holding Bentley for a lift and a spit was almost as good as a hug.

THE WANDERER

Lee attached his favourite lens, the 50mm 1.2, onto his full-frame Canon 6D. He preferred his shots to be all about the subject – tight compositions with no background. It was impossible to know if his subjects were from London, Paris, Rome, New York, Las Vegas or, like this one, Skid Row. It was the eyes those windows to the soul that always drew him.

He walked over to the man and greeted him warmly knowing most of society is only one or two pay checks away from *this* man's situation.

Lee held out a cardboard tray for two. "Hi there, like to share a coffee and a bacon roll with me?"

The man nodded.

He held Lee with his eyes. His eyes bleached-blue molluscs in a shell of prune-like flesh showed no shame, despair, fear or sorrow. If it wasn't for the peeled vitamin D overladen face, the tilled brow and hair spiked and clumped with the styling gel of the street and sleep, his strong, still handsome face had the look of an arctic explorer.

Lee asked, "Okay if I sit next to you on the sidewalk?"

Again, a nod.

They ate in silence.

The man initiated the conversation. "What matters to you, son?"

"I guess the simple things in life and reminding others of our common humanity. What about you?"

"Holding on to my freedom. Possessions imprison a man."

He allowed Lee to take his photo, again with a nod.

The Canon's shutter clicked softly on the man. A kindred human on a journey of self-awareness. Four letters connected them to each other – ATCG. The alphabet of all life. The four base pairs of DNA. No separation, only differentiation and connection. This Lee hoped to capture with the power of his image, along with the words.

Back home in his darkroom, Lee processed the image predominately through dodge and burn to add impact and develop mood to the eyes. The technique allowed him to lighten and darken the luminosity values with silvery mid-tones. He wanted his images to convey the religiosity he felt when taking them, the compassion, the humanness.

Ultimately, the image was all. In the dark, alone, Lee's thoughts wandered. Lee had left knowing neither the man's name nor his story. What he had was the noticing of him, a brief connection and an image for others to see and interpret. If a bond was deeply felt, did we always need to know the who, why, where, when and how? If we notice, remember and cease to judge are we content within the freedom and simplicity not knowing brings?

A phrase popped into his head,

The most precious, life-changing connections are butterfly moments.

He refocused on the photo.

Yes, it was perfect.

8 BALLOON MAN

Mahtouz Bahbah places his hand over his heart.

"*Salamalekoum.*" [Hello]

Welcome to my grim landscape. Do you know the one about the sheep, the duck and the rooster? An eight-minute hot air balloon flight. No, it is not a joke! The year 1783, the courtyard of Versailles, one hundred and thirty French citizens, a king and a queen.

NO? Then perhaps you *know* the one about the Soviets, the Mujahedeen, the Taliban and the US? A forty-year fight.

1978. A beginning with no end. Afghanistan. Death and displacement. One and a half million killed, one million injured, six million refugees and two million internally displaced. Everyday life in Kabul is fear, explosions and grief.

Ah, Kabul! Once the Paris of Asia, today a city of ghosts. Afghanistan is a rubble of a country. A no man's land of ammunition dumps and land mines. Cluster and carpet bombs destroy villages and large areas of forest. We are left with refugees, extreme poverty, drought and polluted air and water.

All I own is how I feel. I carry my God and my nationality inside me. It is the only constant in a time of fear, grief and oppression. Many children know only carpet and walls.

I am a forgiving man who holds hope in his heart.

"*Assalumualaikun.*" [Peace be unto you]

You are yet to understand, 'blood cannot be washed out with blood'. None of you admits 'his own buttermilk is sour'. Why do I stand here looking skyward with balloons of orange, yellow, pink and blue on this November autumn day? It is because I know 'patience is bitter, but its fruit is sweet' and that 'the world decays as hope is devoured'.

In my left hand, I hold the colours of the light. Orange for the spirit. Yellow for faith, humility and truth. Pink for love, joy and renewal. Blue for the water that washes away all sins with wisdom, kindness and peace.

"*Allahu Akbar.*" [God is greatest]

You pursue your agendas and forget what is precious. Is not family sacred to us all?

Look around me. Observe the thousands of graves dotted around the mountain skirt. I stand in Kart-e-Sakhi Cemetery in western Kabul, a place as much for the living as the dead. Street kids hustle for a living, peddlers like me circulate, young lovers seek privacy to speak on their phones, hashish smokers cluster and chat, a student studies as he walks and, on the weekend, cockfights. Here the memory of the dead is kept fresh. It is our custom to pay ten afghanis for others to wash our family graves, and in turn it keeps the stomachs of the living fed, for this will buy an oval naan bread.

The other balloons in Kabul are the 'American kites'. They spy on us with their ever-watchful eyes, reminding us of our oppression. We see them shimmering heavenward in the pale buttermilk daytime haze. At night they become a single light blinking infrared.

I say to you all, forget your incendiaries, bombs and blimps. Drain your oceans, your lakes, your rivers and send to us water balloons, maybe on an autumn day such as this or perhaps in the spring, the season of the rains. Bring water, without the thunder and the lightning, to our wasted land. Wash away your sins. Allow us to forgive, but not forget.

As you place your hand over your heart as you leave, I wait for you to say to such as me ...

"*Mualaikumsalam.*" [Peace also be upon you]

✍ THE TATTOOED SORCERESS

This is a work of historical fiction. Apart from Estefany Cerro Flores, all names are factual.

Time present, time past, time future. I, the eternal one, see them all. Not long ago, you thought me wife, regent, concubine. NO! Wealthy and powerful, I am Moche Priestess Queen. You encase my tattooed body, but I move in the drift of stars.

Entombed in cinnabar earth for one thousand, two hundred years, I am neither flesh nor fleshless. The withered skin on my arms, ankles and feet is inked with the divine – snakes, spiders, crabs, the tree of life and the stars themselves. Always, I am one with the Sky God, Moon Goddess and Mother Earth. As communicator with the gods, I am both protector and sacrificer. You ... you are violators!

You try to understand and redeem time by unredeemable acts of excavation. With care, you excite yourselves as you empty the hidden and disturb the dignified. You do not respect that the divine lives in my skin. I am not a puzzle for you to take apart and measure with forceps and callipers. You place the sacred – my skeleton, my goblet, my rock crystal amulet – into the barren womb of artificial light and prying eyes. I am Priestess Queen. You will know who is weak and who is powerful.

It is June twenty-first, Peru's winter. At a pleasant nineteen degrees centigrade, it is the dry season – the season for tourists, and the day marking the end of the harvest, the winter solstice. The year is 2005.

Tonight, at the Larco Museum in Lima, a distinguished group of forty men gather to pay tribute to their ten years of archaeological investigation and conservation in El Brujo, a recently recognised significant religious capital. Their discovery of the Tomb of Lady of Cao in the El Brujo Pyramid has turned on its head the belief powerful males dominated Mohica society.

The museum has prepared a tour, a presentation and a gourmet dinner inspired by the regional specialities of Peru. Among the guests are Dr Franco Jordan, the lead scientist; his colleague Segundo Vasquez; Dr Guillermo Wiese, owner of Peru's Weise Bank; members of the National Cultural Institute of Lo Libertad who permitted each excavation and members of the National University of Trujillo.

Privately owned, the museum sits in the eighteenth-century vice-royal building built over the ruins of a seventh-century pre-Columbian sacred pyramid. The Larco is a world-renowned museum of pre-Columbian artefacts. The Culture Gallery Hall showcases the people from the north coast of Peru, including the Mochica. The Lady of Cao mummy is on loan, especially for the occasion, from the El Brujo Archaeological Complex. A climate-controlled chamber displays her mummified tattooed body, and a viewing window and mirror allow the body to be seen indirectly.

Franco Jordan has three loves. His work, his wife and gastronomy. He is looking forward to the culinary specialities of the Café del Museo restaurant. As a keen gardener and lover of beauty he has always appreciated the stunning garden setting. Beneath a luscious canopy of ruby-red bougainvillea, trailing bright green vines tendril walls. Below, a kaleidoscope of potted plants and herbaceous borders fringe the entire path to the restaurant area. Everything is lush and beautiful. Not a wilted leaf or spent flower.

It is a cloudless night and the sky is velvet sequinned with stars. There is a light breeze and a feeling of the magic that accompanies eating out in the open air at sunset as dusk straddles dark.

Of all the artefacts, Franco Jordan has two favourites. The first a 'Tumi' – a ceremonial knife with a plain handle and semi-circular blade. The Moche, descendants of the sun god Inti, used it to slit the throats of captives as blood sacrifices in ritual battle. The other is a sizeable inclusion-free pear-shaped cabochon rock crystal drop hung on a necklace of matching beads. His wife would adore it. A similar one is for sale online at Muzeioin Antiquities. For an artefact with pedigree provenance, it's a steal at US$8,500. He'll buy it as a gift for their fifteenth anniversary in July.

Franco Jordan peruses the menu. Peruvian delicacies. Pomme de Terre soufflés with avocado puree. His favourite. His mouth salivates as he thinks of the potato fried till it inflates into delicate balloons. Causa Rellena, a mix of potatoes, chilli and lemon stuffed with octopus and crab pulp. His nostrils and mouth never truly feel free of the desert dust, and he thirsts for a pisco sour, for the delicious assault of brandy with the gentle smoothness of frothy egg whites, and the sweetness of simple syrup balanced by the astringent hint of the fresh lime and angostura bitters.

At six p.m. the meal arrives. Sunset. The waiters remove the lids simultaneously from the dishes on the table where the guests are already seated.

Franco Jordan savours his pisco sour as the zesty brandied liquid filters through the creamy froth. He inhales deeply, lets out an, "Ahhh," and relaxes. As he turns the stem of the glass in his fingers, the contents change to deep red. His first thought is, *a culinary party-trick. How clever.* Curious, he sniffs. The aroma is not familiar. As the contents rise, he swipes the rim of the glass with his index finger, raises the finger to his tongue and licks. He spits into his white napkin, his face a taut mask of disgust and horror. *"My god, it's blood,"* he yells.

Others at the table look in bewildered horror as their drinks morph and overflow without end, turning a white tablecloth red. When the cloth is saturated, blood the consistency of watered-down mucus overflows sticky and shiny onto the floor. Within seconds, the bloody lava clots and stretches over the entire ground.

Instinctively, Franco Jordan's skin crawls, adrenalin pumps, fear sits like indigestion under his ribcage. The air is metallic with blood and fear. It is at this moment the real horror erupts.

The ballooned potatoes spasm and split to release battalions of Goliath tarantulas; their legs air-piano over the ragged edges. Suddenly, blood-curdling screams ejaculate, high-pitched as air is forced roughly out of human lungs. Shrieks thin and sharp like shattered glass add to the confusion and cacophony. Goliaths scatter. Hairs hurled from their abdomens, spear eyes. Now Cyclops's visioned, Franco Jordan screeches as venomed fangs strike downward piercing his flesh and that of those around him. Everywhere is a stampede, frantic chaos and piercing screams, but there is nowhere to run. The floor is a blood-rink. The dining room is a bluster as bodies clamour. Men trample, slip, collide. Chairs scatter like discarded cigarette butts. Everything is amplified impotent panic.

The Causa Rellenos writhe and scuttle as legions of vipers and crabs vie for freedom. The vipers a tangled sea of living spaghetti seasoned with reptilian unblinking eyes. Forked tongues lick the air for the acrid smell of fear. Found, white jaws yawn. Long curved fangs lust for venom into muscle. They strike, holdfast, rendering desperate struggle pointless. Like the others, Franco Jordan is immobilised living prey. The horror and the excruciating pain is trapped in his soundless eyes like a still-life painting. Venom courses through his body. His tissue dissolves into soft pulp – his innards and skin an over-ripe persimmon. His breath is now moist and noisy, his skin mottled. His airways close to asthmatic gasps. Diaphragm cripples. Breath ceases. The air is pungent with the smell of urine and the acetone odour of bodily shutdown.

The scene is now a nocturnal tapestry of bodies encrusted with feasting spiders and snakes. Then come the crabs, iron-rats with massive claws. They are here to claim death's offal. Pick-axe pincers pry open skulls. Frenzied salivating mouths devour brain and strip flesh to sinew and bone.

Those who were living are now dead. As the charcoaled night deepens, the nocturnal predators dematerialise. A sudden earthquake emanates under the pile of death. An adobe brick pyramid with seven sacrificial platforms surrounded by deep pits pushes relentlessly upwards from the earth like a giant whale.

Then, it is all over.

An eerie silence circles and settles in a matter of minutes like a vulture over a carcass. Nocturnal bird sounds cease.

The earth is still and silent.

The Policia National del Peru (PNP) has a reputation as an inconsistent group of individual officers. Some are corrupt and intimidating, others jovial and approachable. Estefany Cerro Flores is the latter. Flores comes from a long line of police officers eager to serve despite the low pay and rampant corruption. She knows with pride that no one in her lineage had ever taken a bribe to bolster their salary. She also prides herself on her response to reported crime – swift and effective.

Three calls went out that evening at six p.m. 106 – medical, for potentially-life threatening situations. 119 – civil defence, earthquakes and natural disasters. 105 – acts of violence. There was no number for supernatural events.

First to arrive at the scene, on her Harley, is Flores. As she approaches, it appears there has been a natural disaster strangely specific to the restaurant area. The only scene it reminds her of is a fire where every home was scorched while one remained untouched. Fate and wind are unpredictable forces. After parking her bike, she scans her flashlight in an arc around the area. After fifteen paces her flashlight arcs skyward.

Blargh.

Bent over, wrists on knees, vomit like finely diced watery vegetable stew propels, sprays and splatters. She dry retches, then gags as caustic bile like long rivulets of yellow snot burn her throat. Through watery eyes she fumbles for her water bottle. She rinses her mouth and boots, but the vile stench and taste linger. Her face is sagged and sallow.

Her Initial Responding Officer Report will be simple – no statements from witnesses or victims. It is a moan-less-massacre. Flores secures the scene and takes out her notebook.

Scattered mutilated bodies, possibly hurled from the top of the pyramid. Deep cuts to bones. Limbs and jawbones ripped from sockets. Severed skulls. Brains missing. Bodies, pale and deflated, indicate draining of blood and tissue. Museum intact. No survivors.

She awaits the crime scene investigation unit.

The CSI unit will discover that the mummy of The Lady of Cao and her artefacts have been stolen and will forever wonder why such carnage was exacted. Even for the cocaine-dealing Ndrangheta mafia, this is dying under mysterious circumstances taken to the extreme.

El Comercio the leading Peruvian daily newspaper will wonder if there is any relevance between 'Cao' and its closeness to the word 'coca', the plant from which cocaine is extracted.

The files will be marked, *asesinato a sangre fria de 53 seres humanos – No Resulto.* They will gather dust and mould, away from prying eyes, till all within them is forgotten.

I am whole. Blood flows through my veins. My once withered skin is plump and my inkings black as ebony. My tumble stone clear rock crystal pendant, the supreme gift of Mother Earth and incarnation of the Divine, is restored to me. You saw power, prestige and ownership in what was not yours to take. To me, the pendant is, and has always been, and will always be, the gateway to my divine powers.

Healing.

Meditation.

Clarity and strength of thought.

Expansion of consciousness.

Meant to be with me in life and death, it is guide and protector. Without it my spirit is restless.

You would do well to remember we are the weavers of our destiny. As the Creator does, so does the spider, the crab and the snake. How dare you name me Lady of Cao!

I am Moche Priestess Queen, and I live in the drift of stars.

ℐ RIP

Do you know an Adidas Diablo duffel bag has a volume of approximately ten litres and a capacity of ten kilos? That's £100,000, in hundred-pound notes, stacked in bundles of ten thousand or, if need be, a dachshund called Snags.

Cecilia, a not-so-innocent bystander; Rodney Robinson, a not-so-bright petty criminal and Cal Savage, a local crime boss (also known as Grimm) are living testimony to the saying bad things happen in threes.

I'm nineteen. I'm out of work … again. Hence the housesitting. As for confessions, I'm a chocoholic. The Betty Crocker, triple chocolate cake type – an innocent but fattening addiction. At this very moment I feel like a homicidal criminal. If only I'd googled theobromine earlier, I'd never have fed him those two squares of unsweetened baking chocolate. Poor Snags. Unnecessary suffering on eight counts:

vomiting, diarrhoea, urinary incontinence, hyperactivity, excessive panting, muscle tremors, seizure and coma.

I read once about a woman given a four-month prison sentence for killing a dog, and that was only on two counts of causing unnecessary suffering. Four multiplied by four is sixteen: incarcerated for 1.333 years. At least I won't worry about providing for my basic needs. I feel wretched with guilt and fear. It would've been kinder if Snags had been run over by a car; it's the reason I give to his owner when I ring him.

"If only he hadn't chased the rabbit in the park. If it had been less furry and not so fast, he might have stood a chance. I am so very, very sorry."

"Look, dear, he was my late wife's dog, and at eighteen he's had a fair innings. At least he died doing what he loved – hunting the closest thing to a badger."

I burst into tears. Death. A lie. The shame.

"Please don't fret, Cecilia, these things happen. Take him to the nearest pet crematorium. Please tell them to cremate him alone, as my wife would have wanted that. I'll sort out everything else when I'm back in a few days."

After the phone call, I pack Snags in my Adidas duffel bag. Ten kilos (including packaging) of adorable, lovable gentle brownness. The Waterloo tube is seriously tinned sardines. I stand by the door with the bag at my feet. As the doors close, a tubeidiot decides to jump on, nearly hobbling me as he drops his duffel bag to the floor. No apologies. It's the worst day ever. Tears well in my eyes again.

You know you're in deep shit if the local crime kingpin asks you, "Do you know who I am?" I do fucking know who he is. Cal Savage. He's a mean motherfucker – small and wiry with narrow eyes and thin lips. "Sure, you own this pet burning gig."

"Correct, Rodney. I run this place."

Cal nods to the burly guy in the corner, his standover man Vince.

Vince dumps the Adidas duffel bag at my feet. There's the sneaking suspicion I've fucked up again.

"I ain't taken nothing out, honest, Cal. It come straight from the tube to here."

"Open it, son," he says slowly and icily.

What the fuck! It's a dead dog!

"What you don't know, Rodney, is I own Oink, the largest pig farm in the area. Pigs, lactating sows to be precise, the best way to disappear a body. Speedy and thorough. Greedy buggers! They go through bone and sinew like bread-and-butter pudding. Of course, Vince here will shave your head and pull your teeth out first. Don't want to make it too hard on their digestion. What do you think, Vince? Fourteen? It'll be *hasta la vista* for our Rodney in an hour. Now, where's the fucking money?"

I'm in deep shit.

I am so bait.

Vince leaves the room, and I expect him to return with a razor and pliers. He doesn't.

He returns empty-handed and whispers into Cal's ear.

A whisper saves my fucking life.

I ain't *never* gonna stuff up again.

Talk about the hymn 'Amazing Grace', that under-brained punk Rodney was fucking lucky. I'd left the room to fetch the razor and pliers when Sal our receptionist called me aside.

"Just had a teenaged girl with a dachshund to drop off for this afternoon's cremation. Steve was about to take it out of the duffel bag before putting it in the unit. Cal needs to know, forget about 1400 degrees Fahrenheit for this little bundle. There's one hundred thousand pounds in here."

8 BUDDHA'S BUTTERFLY

Nine o'clock, and I said I'd be there by ten. Much of the time my life's a transit lane between appointments and my days lengthy sentences with semi-colons. *I'm hungry.* I spot it when I reach the crest of the road.

Should I?

Shouldn't I?

My brain's always a telephone exchange of thoughts and internal dialogue. I'm aghast when it becomes external in public places. I know the look I get and hear their thoughts: Oh, she must live on her own.

Anyway, although it is on the corner on my side of the road, I keep on driving.

Just do it.

Do it!

My body needs a dash of nourishment and my soul a soupcon of spontaneity. I turn off at the nearest side road and, as I do a U-turn, my entire body is a toasted marshmallow smile. Alongside the café the tarmac-imprisoned earth breaks free into a crumble of caramel and a chiffonade of green. I park. The horizon is peek-a-boo ocean through the greenery and the air a hallelujah of crispness and salt.

Inside, all is woodland-industrial chic and paned natural light. A timber ledge follows the length of the window that overlooks the road. The stools are hard and high. Not wanting to feel like a baby in a highchair I scan for the nearest table and chairs. The menu disappoints. The pot of tea I order – ginger, turmeric and lemongrass – contains a bland haystack in a stainless-steel weir. My palate craves infused zested fleshy surrender of rhizome and peel. Dried is not for the sensualist; it is for the lazy or those who can't obtain. In this trendy seaside hub, there is no excuse. No salad, vegetables or leafy garnish. Is the menu uninspired or a war on waste? Or maybe they don't want Dorothy to find the end of the rainbow.

Food is art. It is colour, aroma, taste, sound, texture and artful arrangement in perfect balance. All that is in exile. The meal is drab mushrooms with snail-trails of aioli. The sourdough toast looks apologetic and unconfident of its pedigree. Steamrolled to thinness, only the crust and the yeasty air pockets protest, *Believe me, I AM sourdough!* My fault too. I ordered smoked salmon as a side when it needed bacon. My hunger and the explorer in me satisfied, I leave knowing I will never return.

After my appointment I go for an ocean swim on the incoming tide where the creek opens its mouth to the sea. Tucked around the corner from the main beach is a beach fit for three. It's a weekday and I have it all to myself. I stretch out on my towel and close my eyes. My sun-glowed skin's a recharging battery as gentle bejewelled glints flicker through the weave of my straw sunhat onto closed eyelids. My thoughts drift to a true story, long unrecalled but worth remembering. It carries me with it like the returning tide. It is the story of Little Buddha and Schmetterling.

Forty years ago (the eighties), my life and their story coincided over two elemental forces of nature – ice and lava. One, a spherical shrine of hollowed ice sheltering marinated shrimp with sea urchin and caviar, on a bed of sea lettuce. The other, a dessert with floating islands of fluffy hazelnut meringue lapped by pools of vanilla praline cream and marbled (when spoon breached meringue) by languid lava rivulets of raspberry and dark chocolate coulis.

Tekeshi and Theo. Their births separated by fifteen years and an ocean; their childhoods conjoined by isolation. Adulthoods guided by the call for fusion of culture, community and cuisine.

The Pacific Ocean calls, familiar and unfamiliar. Dunes and turtles fringe the coastal city where Tekeshi lives. Hamamatsu. A city charmed with a sixteenth-century castle, four hundred cherry trees and a cocktail-layered vista of white, blue and green. The mammoth Mount Fuji (four thousand metres tall, elegant and snow-capped) embraces what lies below like a friendly uncle. The area is culture and nature-rich – shrines, waterfalls, volcanic foothills and a linear landscape of rowed plantations of green tea. In Utogi, wasabi grows in the sacred meltwaters from Mount Fuji that produce the clear streams of the Fuji, Oi and Abe Rivers. In Suruga Bay the rare delicately sweet sakura shrimp float and scatter.

Tekeshi's family are rural people, and his favourite dish is gyoza: unassuming yielding dumpling pockets whose feminine softness and warmth allow the attention of taste buds to the flavour and texture inside. Always for Tekeshi the soy to add tang and depth and the freshly-shaved local wasabi for a quickly fading heat that sears the nostrils and waters the eyes of the unseasoned naïve eater. Who could not help but smile after a comforting belly full of gyoza? The known means little to Tekeshi. What tugs at him like a child wanting attention is the call of the *unknown* – a desire to experience a foreign fusion of bush and city. His parents with their *umeboshi* (sour plum) faces and toil-hardened veined hands cannot understand this desire in their only child and, because they do not understand, he is not close to them. Their outlook on life is like the dumpling without the filling. No tang of soy sauce. No heat of the wasabi. Not wanting an answer, they ask him in Japanese, "Why do you go?"

The sharp slap of silence.

"You stop your studies, and you will be alone with no money and no job."

Their words will change nothing.

In-between his business management studies, Tekeshi works early mornings and late nights as a kitchen porter in a hotel. He saves enough to qualify for a twelve-month Working Holiday Visa in Australia. He is twenty.

It is five-thirty p.m. in Sydney, the time when daylight skulks slowly away under the slate-grey of early evening. It's the hiatus between the day's mix of the ordinary and the evening's diverse incomings of the bright and the tarnished; the slick and the refined; the feather-bowered and the sequined; the addled, addicted and androgynous; the bisexuals, metrosexuals and transsexuals; the bohemians, cross-dressers, models, socialites and paper bag metholics. This nocturnal family of the fun-hungry (apart from the methylated) will queue in long snaking lines to enter the burnt orange, sage green and cream Art Deco building that stands majestically on the corner of the nightclub precinct. All of them drawn, in order of importance, by sex, theatre, food, art and politics.

On the opposite corner is the real estate office of Ari Finkler. Theo Nilsson has popped in for a hi-and-bye catch-up.

"Mazel tov on your latest venture, Theo. Restaurant, nightclub, cabaret theatre, bar, brasserie. You heff no fear. You open more restaurants than most people heff sex."

"I think you need to speak to your wife about that one, Ari. The average is once a week. I know you're a true gentleman, but it would help if you told her to *shtup* regularly." It's an in-joke. Theo was highly amused the day he discovered something that sounded like *shut up* meant *to have sex* in Yiddish.

"Better now I tell you a joke, Theo. Heff I told you de one about Simon?"

"You probably have, Ari, but they're always worth a third hearing, old chap."

"It's Simon's ninetieth birthday. Miriam stands at de bedroom door in a new negligee. She dims the light, and says, 'Heff I got sumtink for you, Simon – Super Sex.' He replies, 'Vunderful. Denk you, darlink.

I'll heff de soup.' You shake your head, Theo. Tomorrow I have new joke for you."

Theo worries about Ari's repetitive repertoire of jokes always full of hyperbole and nuanced complaint. Ari worries about Theo's *big plans*. Plans with the grand vision, impulsivity and foolhardiness of an alcoholic. For all his brilliance as a chef, Theo is a *lechen kopt* – a noodlehead – when it comes to business. Still, his evangelical zeal, passion, kindness and warm-hearted chutzpah make strangers feel like family and rarely fail to draw sponsors and business partners. Ari knows. He is one of them. He has a half-share in the corner building across the road. Poor Theo, thinks Ari. Sometimes wrong place, wrong time. The man has as much introspection as a Jack Russell.

Tekeshi arrives at Sydney airport. Booking an airport shuttle is still too demanding for his low-level English. He sticks with the simplicity of what he knows – trains. He has no plan where to alight. He's already run into trouble asking a person who has an inner seat next to them, "Prease, I shit?" Ignored, he wonders if this culture knows little about politeness.

St James station. The train empties. Tekeshi takes this as his cue; besides, it's the third stop and three is his lucky number. Once in daylight he's at the place where concrete paths act as compass points as they corral one of the oldest parks in Australia. He marvels at the wide-open space, the lush grass surrounded by buildings and busy roads with relays of buses. He sits on a bench and contentedly soaks up the last of the late afternoon sun's rays then, as the sun sinks, he wanders towards a large and impressive fountain. He wonders if it has carp. No carp.

Instead, a six-metre pedestalled bronze statue of a lean muscular youth whose right arm extends protectively and, in his left, a stringed musical instrument. Beneath the figure, water falls from the nostrils of horse heads into tri-levelled granite basins and from there into a pool of stone dolphins and tortoises who expel jets of water. A god. A goat. A goddess and her stag. A drawn sword and a horned beast.

Tekeshi waits till the light fades and the magic of floodlights illuminate. He marvels at the detail and the scale of the fountain but prefers the works of Akio Makigawa whose contemporary sculptures capture the elemental forces of nature with tranquil stillness and dynamism. Sculptures not to subdue or impress but to invite connection and contemplation.

He wanders through the park and takes the path that leads him to an easterly road. It seems the one most likely to lead him away from the hubbub and expensive hotels.

Theo gone, Ari Finkler is about to close shop and set the alarm. Already the chill of the night air insinuates, biting into the lingering warmth left by the air-con. He's about to switch the lights off when he sees, in the transparent space between the ads, the smooth round-as-a-ball face of a man with small set eyes with single-edged eyelids. Another Japanese tourist lost without translation. Ari watches with amusement as the eyes scour, first the 'For Sale' and then 'To Let'. The man looks placidly puzzled as he draws up the zippered collar of his black anorak. Ari waits for the zeros to drop.

A mild panic rises in Tekeshi's chest. He realises everything in the window has too many zeros for his wallet. *Where is he going to stay tonight?*

Ari taps on the window and beckons him in. "Hello, I'm Ari Finkler."

"Herro, my name Tekeshi Tanaka."

"You look like you need help."

"Justa momentu prease …" He tries to repeat Ari's words. "Ooh rooko rike—"

"Vait. Vait," Ari interrupts in staccato. Ari draws a giant question mark in the air with his index finger, shrugs his shoulders and places both palms upwards from bent arms, his eyes wide and his brow furrowed. Tekeshi yawns, tilts his head to the right and places his hands in prayer position against his right cheek. Then, he does the most unexpected and outrageous thing of all. He closes his eyes as a series of snores rattle from his nose and throat in a sleep apnea duet. *Somewhere to sleep.* Caught between comprehension and astonishment, Ari bellows with laughter and immediately knows he likes this man and his innocent happy energy. Tekeshi slowly opens one eye and smiles a smile of the understood. Ari's already thought of a nickname for him. Little Buddha.

"You tourist?"

"One more."

"Holiday? Verk Visa?"

"Yesu ... horidy walk bisa. Back Tokyo, walk hoteru."

Ari knows where he is going to take him. To someone whose familial, supportive, embracing mentorship needs a kitchen porter. "You vill please come mit me."

Ari and Little Buddha cross the road with the same technique: find a gap in the two-way lanes, walk in a brisk straight line, look straight ahead. Those who waiver end up humiliated, maimed or dead. Cornered by the constant honk and hum of two roads and abutted by buildings either side is a two-storey Art Deco building with two façades, one facing south, the other east. Tekeshi and Ari appraise the building very differently.

Ari knows it well. On his books for an eight-figure sum eighteen months before, he and Theo own a fifty percent share each. In its heyday it would have listed as POA – Price On Application. Apart from the incredible twelve-foot-high ceilings and an impressive central foyer that rises two storeys, he dislikes the building: it is an ill-matched mishmash of styles. Due to a lack of maintenance, unsympathetic aluminium replacements embarrass the original 1930s arched double-hung windows with timber sashes. Blocked-in second floor windows shame the decorative mouldings from the 1950s. The final act of vandalism is the latest addition to the first floor, a cantilevered balcony with a timber deck and toughened clear glass.

Ari thinks, *Oy vey! Oy vey!* But he says, "You like? Beautiful?"

Tekeshi nods politely, "Byuutifuru."

What Tekeshi sees is quite different. He sees beyond the building to the flow of energy around it. He sees it as an island and the roads as rivers whose speed has cutting energy, a place of business bound by the power of two roadways forming an L-shape that attracts a steady stream of people, but all of them burdened by petty troubles. The southern second-storey windows have their eyes blinded; board replaces glass. No looking outside. No looking within.

The building's entrance faces east and above the doorway on the stucco is a sign in substantial neon letters – ABELLAS. A broad hedged pedestrian walkway that hides the road from sight but not sound is a functional solution lacking in elegance. Overall, Tekeshi knows Abellas will be a place where the money is tidal – difficulties and struggles in forming a solid business footing. Easy beginnings. Difficult continuings. The building's street number contains two threes and an eight. $3 + 3 + 8 = 14$ and $1 + 4 = 5$. Five means prosperity will flow but also agitation and bad luck. The man who owns this has come for growth and validation but also to find inner peace and balance. An old Japanese proverb pops into Tekeshi's head. He who runs after two hares will catch neither.

As Ari and Tekeshi enter the foyer, each feels the dramatic impact of space and largess. Wide fluted cornices border the twelve-foot ornate geometric ceiling. A leadlight Art Deco sun rises two-storeys through the centre of the foyer and is flanked, on the wall either side, by a seven-foot Artes-style bronze sculpture of a dancer and an outrageously large colourful advert for the 1985 Sydney Gay Mardi Gras.

"It's wow. Yes?"

"Wao," repeats Tekeshi, but the bold geometric diamonds, the triangles and the angular lines unsettle him. They look like shards and spear-tips meant to cut and slice.

The foyer's amber-glass doors lead to a lift that they take to the first floor. As they alight a door faces them. It belongs to a small two-bedroom flat, a modification to allow the head-chef to sleep over on the busiest nights that finish for patrons at one-thirty in the morning and for him with sunrise, the last of the previous night's wine and then, bed. The door is slightly ajar, and Ari calls out, "Schmetterling, come and meet Little Buddha."

Theo and an oversize glass of a 1978 Chateau Latour come to the door. He is still in his head chef's white and black. "Ari, old chap, will you stop calling me that. The word sounds like something that could do serious damage."

Theo is wary of any of Ari's *schm* words as, apart from *schmetterling*, they are all pejoratives: *schmutzig* (dirty), *schmuck* (self-made fool, aka dick), *schmoe* (a stupid person), *schmoppet* (a charming puppet with a limited vocabulary).

"Vell, my old friend, I promise dat ven you stop acting like a butterfly." The reference is to Theo's signature yellow bow tie, alongside his compulsive flits from one new restaurant venture to another seeking the nectar of success.

"His real name, Ari?"

"Tekeshi."

Theo turns to Tekeshi and bows slightly. He knows Ari's brought him another kitchen hero. The man deserves a finder's fee. "Hello, I'm Theo. Nice to meet you."

"Me too."

It's an exchange between two faces whose default position is generosity and warmth.

"Why don't you work for me?"

"One more prease."

Theo realises it's the 'don't' that has confused him. He points, "*You.* Work for *me.*"

"Ah, yesu! I walk you."

Theo waves them both inside. "Here's a red for you, Ari. Tekeshi?

"No, prease."

Ari swirls and sniffs the red as he holds the large rounded bowl by the stem, but he's not concentrating on the scent or the closing note of the wine's aroma. He takes a small sip and allows it to roll around on his tongue for a moment. "I em vundering–"

"Wondering if it's okay if he could stay here in the second bedroom till he's on his feet," Theo adds before Ari can finish.

"You know me too vell, my friend."

"Look, Ari, old chap, you've always been a person of small kindnesses. Without you at boarding school, at the age of six, I'd have been lobster mousse within a day."

Ari raises his glass, "L'chayim, chaver. To life, my friend."

"To life and friendship, Ari. To you too, Tekeshi."

Within two weeks Tekeshi has mastered the rhythm of a professional kitchen. He's preemptive, strategic, quick on his feet, spatially aware and energetic. He's cool around heated chefs and cookpots and on top of everything: speed of cleaning pots, pans and tools and homing them in the right place so they're ready to go. The floor is spotless. Food is peeled and chopped with lightning precision and the needs of the various chefs preempted. Theo and the kitchen staff have created a nickname for him. Ninja Octopus.

Teasing Tekeshi eases the pressure in the kitchen. He gives as good as he gets.

"Where is the butter, Tek?"

"Re/frig/er/a/tor."

"What do you need to do with the cake?"

"Dekorehshan keki."

Then there's his pronunciation of McDonalds (Ma/kudo/na/ru/do), and the light banter finds the larrikin in him, and he shouts out alongside the kitchen staff and chefs, "Oi. Oi. Oi." It's a refrain that crosses seamlessly between national borders. Seemingly unpronounceable Japanese words to the Western eye and tongue – *tsutaerarenakatta* (couldn't tell), *occhokochoi* (clumsy) and *atatakakunaketta* (wasn't warm) – redress the balance of vocal incompetencies.

Curious and watchful as well as playful, Tekeshi pinpoints Theo's style: respectful to the rhythm of the seasons; pure, clean flavours; bold and exotic combinations and brilliantly aesthetic platings. All the dishes have a casually absolute elegance and joy. Theo is equally watchful. Within six months he asks Tekeshi, "I want to introduce a new selection to the pre-theatre degustation menu. Sushi. Are you okay to do that, Tekeshi? Samples by the end of the month."

"Mmm. No problem," Tekeshi says with calm assuredness, as the first step in his plan does not include washing dishes forever, but he's thinking, *why people berieve if you Japanese, you eat sushi, you make it?* He has done neither. His calm exterior betrays none of the flutters he feels in his chest. Flutters like a small bird trapped in a bamboo cage.

It's fifteen months since Theo opened Abellas as head chef and part-owner. He is peeling under the pressure of the physical challenge of a 19/6 week that feels like 24/7, the rigid schedules, the responsibility, the unknown, the financial risk. He feels trapped. The puritan in him reaches for the hedonist to relieve the drive for perfection, to drown the fear of not being good enough, of tumbling from the firmament of his restaurant's coveted three hats and of being voted Restaurant of the Year but with only one of the three possible hats.

First comes the Grand Marnier – the remnants left in a bottle after the night's souffles. When there is not enough in the bottle, another is opened. Unlike red wine, Theo is not improving with time. His structural faults are maintained and accentuated. His favourites increase from Bollingers at two hundred dollars a bottle to Jean-Louis Chave Hermitages at five hundred. Until the night he opens his cellar's most expensive bottle, a Gros Père et Fils, Grand Cru Richebourg. Seven thousand dollars. He begins to argue with himself.

Sober: *Oh no, Theo.* You'll go broke.

Sloshed: *So what?* Highs and lows. Penury's never permanent.

Sober: *You're an alcoholic!* Admit it, old chap, you need help.

Sloshed: *Bugger off!* I'm a dignified, disinclined to violence, drunk.

Sober: *How the hell would you know?* You can't remember what you did last night.

Drinking buddies: "It'll be OK, mate. Have a drink."

Theo's committed to three packets of unfiltered Camels a day, each cigarette fourteen milligrams of tar and one milligram of nicotine. His day begins with three cigarettes when he's half-asleep and still in bed as he thinks about the day ahead. Another cigarette when he goes to the loo and then, one after showering.

Tekeshi no longer lives in the flat, so he's not witness to the squatters scattered like knocked-over skittles: bottles of wine partially and fully emptied. Spills next to the bed and on the coffee table, and an overflow of empties in sink and bin, further betray Theo. As alcohol is nothing without food, and food nothing without alcohol, the debris from slices of truffle on croutons and artisanal blue cheeses on fig and olive specialty crackers means Theo's a pre-poster boy for AA and Weight Watchers.

What Tekeshi does notice when they are together in the restaurant kitchen is Theo's aftershave – a pungent mix of kitchen, alcohol and tobacco. Theo's, "Fix it", reprimands to the other chefs when platings are not up to standard are frayed and inconsistent. His bow tie is having a nervous breakdown. It no longer sits flat and central. It's skewered and its left-top corner buckles under a wayward collar. On the worst of days, it's a crumpled origami butterfly salvaged from a wastepaper bin. Theo's already delicate hair is thinning on top like wisps of wind-blown candyfloss. That his socks don't match is not a fashion statement. Overall, he has the wayward look of an absent-minded professor.

Tekeshi has the deep calm of a fisherman, but he is unable to lead Theo by example: tai chi, relaxing breathing techniques, meditation and fishing. Theo is too driven – all movement, and no space. Worried for Theo, Tekeshi, at the end of one of his shifts, pops across the road to see Ari. He takes with him a few samplers he's been experimenting with on his days off. A miniature tuna tart with mustardy wasabi and ginger and carpaccio of scallop on top of foie gras, with citrus dressing.

"Thenk you. Tek a seat. Always gutt to see you, Little Buddha, food or no food."

"I hope you like. Prease, I ask you something?"

"Sure. Vat is it?"

"Ari, I worry about Theo. He is Shinkansen – bullet train." He tells Ari about the tell-tale bow tie.

"My father hed daily ritual. He began de day by making his bed perfectly. He never missed a morning. I dink he vas honouring his day – *If my bed is neat, my day vill be calm and ordered.* Even ven very sick he still made it, but it was never as neat. One day, I am looking into his room, and de bed is not made. Dat day I grieve de most."

Tekeshi honours the silence that follows. He gives Ari time to bring himself into the present.

"Little Buddha, neither of us can put de kibosh on it. He is Mister Perpetual Motion."

"What makes him this?"

"Can't help it. To stop is pain. De pain of regret, guilt and fear for past failures and those he feels he has let down. Mebbe he needs a therapist. He's alvays been ahead of his time, more artist and innovator dan businessman. Dat's vhy he admires and respects you, Tekeshi. You heff all three."

The day after the sushi directive, Tekeshi wakes with a plan. Over the ensuing weeks he samples fifty dishes at the top five sushi trains: Double Bay, Five Dock, Coogee, Randwick, Chatswood. He watches the chefs slice, dice, roll, cook and sculpt. Within the month he presents Theo with a seven-dish degustation menu with a suggested set-price of one hundred and twenty-five dollars. He's also been working on two spectacular dishes at home. One *umami* (savoury), one *amai* (sweet). Both are innovative and elegantly spectacular – *ice and lava*. Tekeshi spends weeks perfecting each delicate, gentle freezing and each chocolate and raspberry rivulet. The two surprise dishes are to match the theme of an upcoming theatre booking. The show, *Elemental*. Theo has entertainment nightly in the restaurant, brasserie and cocktail bar. Tekeshi marvels at his generosity. He's given the theatre booking to a local dance company for a couple of months to help with their cash flow, to rescue them from liquidation.

At midnight, at the end of the first trial evening of the sushi-inspired degustation menu, Theo calls Tekeshi into the restaurant to a round of applause. "To Tekeshi, the master of small things."

At that moment, Tekeshi knows he has found his *ikigai* – his purpose in life.

Theo continues, "No more sink for you, Ninja Octopus. You are now Chef de Partie. Many chefs start in the kitchen. I did myself. In another six months when you finish here, I want you to work for GC's restaurant, Amicus. He's the one that's put Hobart on the gastronomic map. You'll love it. You'll love Tasmania. Pristine waters, fertile soil and an untouched landscape. It's a place above and beyond organic."

Six years and over one thousand kilometres and the Tasman Sea have separated Tekeshi and Theo, but it does not diminish their deep friendship. Tekeshi is now head chef of his own restaurant – Buddha's Butterfly.

Built into the rock face, the architecture and the landscape meld as one. In a riverside setting on the bend of a deep estuary, the building is invisible from a distance. As patrons arrive by a small wooden private ferry, they see Buddha's Butterfly appears like a mirage. The approach clears the mind. It whispers with the balm of a soft breeze, "Leave the chaos and pressure of the outside world behind."

Inside, there are no white box interiors. Sculptures by Makigawa intersperse the raw, natural space. The chopsticks are freshly cut bamboo and are cool in the hands, the lacquerware is warm and the hand-thrown rice bowls feather-light. Day or night, the restaurant holds a subtle, elegant Zen ambience. The restaurant's floor-to-ceiling window embraces the full magnificence of a Japanese garden designed to be viewed on the diagonal and seen optimally from a seated position. Space and scale are transformed, from the hundred-metre mark beyond the garden, by borrowed landscape from a dense and rugged white-trunked bushland tangle of eucalypts.

It is the time of year when day and night are in equal measure. Autumn. Shadow and light, picture and poem, the outside is living art: the glowing golds, rusty reds and ochre orange of autumnal maples; the yellow, copper, bronze and red of Japanese elms; tresses of languorous willows; slender and smooth feathery bamboo; untormented pines and the dark limbs of plum trees. Moss blankets the earth instead of grass, and lichen mottles the large grey stone boulders planted with pleasing random asymmetrical precision. The air is so pure, it is scentless. Its chill forewarns that winter is fast approaching. Yellow, orange, white and red brocaded koi glide and gleam in the pure spring-fed stream that flows westward. A waterfall and a cascade, half-hidden in the shade, flow with a hypnotic rhythm of murmurs and whispers. At night the water catches the magic of the moon's reflection to an audience of hushed voices and muted background music.

Tonight, the clouds blanket the refrigerated air. The nature of change means nothing lasts forever. Winter will soon strip bare, and the lilting mournful trill of the cuckoo will die till its summer return. Tekeshi waits. Waits for the call he knows will come. He waits as a silvery silent mist settles, turning the visible, invisible. It is not a call that arrives but a telegram. A telegram from Ari – *Theo's weak. Come see him ASAP.* Tekeshi takes the first flight. Within three hours he is at Theo's bedside.

Theo opens his eyes for a moment and looks at Tekeshi. Tekeshi takes his hand, and in a gentle voice he says, "You are, and will always be, in every dish I make." They look at each other. Tekeshi smiles but only Theo's eyes speak a smile because his mouth cannot. Death clouds his eyes. Tekeshi will remember Theo's death as *karoshi*, death by a dark word. Overwork. Theo is forty-five.

Sun-dried and sandy I trace my path back to my car on the headland. The waves frill and curl gently to the beach and glide bubble-edged across the moist glazed sand where earth meets water and water meets the azure of the endless sky. I ask myself, why now? Why now, did this story whisper to be told? It called to remind me of what I am not. I am not: the no song of a bird that will not return; the no of the tea that disappointed; the no of the salmon instead of the bacon or the no of unartful plating. It called to remind me of what I am. I am the yes of the vital missing ingredient, a friend to share a spontaneous moment in connection, laughter and banter. That, yes that, would have made all the difference to the start of my day.

♂ ... NOTHING BUT ...

I'm Kamison Kaos. Yesterday's news snippet in the paper, 'Carjack Couple Charged', well, it scissored the truth. I'm a close acquaintance of Noah and Janine and believe me, they're no Bonnie and Clyde! I'd ask you not to assume from my surname that I'm here to create mayhem. I'm here to put the story straight. Reconstructing the damaged must be done quickly whether it's a reputation or hair; otherwise, it's unsalvageable.

First, a bit about me. As far as scissors go, I'm a hair-stylist's eye candy – sleek, handsome and beautifully proportioned. I know my worth. At one hundred and ninety-nine dollars per inch, it's precisely, nine hundred and ninety-nine dollars.

Allegedly.

Don't you love that word? It covers a multitude of false accusations, innuendos and rumours. Blows smoke where there isn't fire. Ultimately, any unfortunate event is a series of unfortunate events. In this case misunderstood youthful exuberance, irresponsible journalism and lazy policing.

I was there when it all happened. Bystander. Impartial witness. My memory is pure, high-grade stainless steel and as ironclad as DNA. Unfortunately, instead of being called as a witness, I was bagged, sealed and silenced.

Frankly, it was an insult to be bagged like an underbelly half-caste knife or blade. Me, threaten, slash, shear or stab? *No way!* I belong to an elite family name that's up there with the Samurai and Zen masters. Google me if you don't believe me. Guess I shouldn't have expected more when the pure meaning of 'scissor' has been sullied by adding '-ing', debasing its nobility to acts such as wrestling, lesbian sex and the making of tortillas. *Please!*

What I share with you is a proxy for my day in court, and you, the reader, will be judge and jury in the comforts of home without subjection to press-gang tactics and low remuneration. And to those of you who've avoided your civic duty by presenting to the pre-jury selection with either a brown-bagged bottle, pearls and a twinset or a copy of Einstein's *Relativity: The Special and the General Theory* – shame on you.

Exhibit A – Carjacking on NSW south coast. Friday night. Mount Pleasant Way.

Either you've got no idea where Nowra is or you do and already hitch a bunch of assumptions about its population and Noah and Janine: no skills, poor work ethic, unreliable, unethical, drug and alcohol dependent, prior convictions, threatening behaviour, carjacking. *Guilty! Guilty!* in flashing neon lights. Sorry, but as you will discover later (Exhibit B), any assumptions you've formed will make an arse of you.

Nowra has fifteen wineries. This may be a worry or may simply mean it has a bustling commercial centre. Youth unemployment is six percent above the national average. The town birthed a bawdy stand-up comedian with the stage name Rodney Rude. This further degraded its reputation. To balance things out, it provided sporting heroes, artists, even an opera singer *and* the winner in the first Melbourne Cup in 1861.

Exhibit B – Noah and Janine

Noah and Janine are sweeties. Like two peas in a pod. Straight dark hair, duckling fine. Almond eyes flecked with light. Their features are small and slightly wonky. In fact, they're delightfully dysmorphic. Before birth, a bad-arsed chromosome decided to show for the party uninvited – like the wicked fairy in *Sleeping Beauty* – mistakes it for a twenty-first and then like all gate crashers causes havoc. Imagine a party with forty-seven presents where forty-six would have done. The spell cast? Down syndrome, aka Trisomy 21.

On paper Noah and Janine are thirty and thirty-four, but add those two numbers together and that's their individual IQ scores. Mild intellectual disability. Imagine them as eight to nine-year-olds

– god love 'em. What they lack in complex reasoning and judgement they make good with their exuberant, affectionate and creative personalities. Put on *Grease*'s 'You're the One That I Want' or *Saturday Night Fever*'s 'Staying Alive' and they're naturals. If you've ever been fortunate enough to fly first class, your paths have crossed. They pack the airline travel bags in a sheltered workshop. They pack all things including nails but, although they can count, they've no concept of number. The highest denomination Janine handles? Fifty dollars. Not once has anyone short-changed her. This warms her mum's heart.

Exhibit C – *Ahmed Matar, taxi owner & driver*

Mr Matar a Punjabi with barely passable English left himself on the side of the road – more about the why, later. His testimony should be scissored from the record as ill-founded hysteria.

Although industrious, he has a string of known convictions as the originator of two hundred and forty-three fraudulent Taxi Transport Subsidy Scheme vouchers – fare rebates from the State Government for disabled passengers.

To Dhanmeet Matar, disabled meant missing or immobilised body parts and cumbersome wheelchairs. He'd never had the likes of Noah and Janine as passengers, and the way they looked, talked and were slow to answer made him uneasy and frightened.

Concluding Statement

I was in this unfolding of events, as Janine's sister has a low-stress hair salon on the Central Coast. I belong to Melissa, and Janine and Noah were bringing me back from the scissor sharpener in town. Melissa's salon is for those with any disability or sensory issues. No-no's in the salon are bright lights, overwhelming wall art, loud music and noisy hairdryers. Where upmarket salons offer you champagne or a custom-made coffee and biscuits, she provides talc about the neck and swimming googles. Make an appearance in flippers or a superhero outfit and she is thrilled.

What the paper didn't reveal was that the case was later dismissed on appeal.

What I'm about to tell you is the whole truth and … nothing but …

Janine took me out of the box to show Noah, precisely when Matar's radio decided to play a tribute to John Travolta and Olivia Newton-John. To cut a long story short, Noah and Janine began singing discordantly in the back, scissors in hand, executing the moves to the best of their ability in a confined space. The combination of 'Staying Alive' and their imposed rhyming with the year, 1995, was all too much. In fear for his life, Matar panicked and fled the taxi with the underlying feeling bad karma had eventually decided to check in. Failure to put on the handbrake meant the car took off to a steady roll on the slope of the road till it came to a slow and smooth halt on the flat, and that is where the sniffer dogs found Noah, Janine and myself dancing and singing on the roadside to 'You're the One That I Want'.

By way of a happy footnote, all charges were later dropped, and Dhanmeet Matar admitted in his own words, "This mistake has been making of me."

Dhanmeet Matar remains industrious but has chosen the path of an ethical man – a man with enough compassion to embrace the feel of talc on his neck every few months.

♉ THE BFF

Every morning a crow comes and sits at my window. I've already prepared the delicacies he will eat from my flattened palm. He announces himself with a single tap on the pane like a guest who knows his presence is always welcome to enliven an ordinary day.

How did our friendship come about? With crumbs. I was a sloppy eater. A four-year-old is usually forgiven for such a misdemeanour of manners unless she has an older brother.

"Mu-um, Gabi's got crumbs everywhere again!" For that reason, Jude never sat next to me when Mum collected him from school with me in tow.

"It's her small rosebud mouth," Mum would explain. "Go easy on her."

"I never did *that* at her age. *It's disgusting!*"

"No, you didn't," Mum stated matter-of-factly, "but you did avoid wiping your own bottom until you were quite old."

That shut him up.

The crumbs always fell away from me when, arriving home, I got out of the car. That alone is how my friendship developed with a crow. I had difficulty with the 'cr' sound, and that is why crow became, and remained, 'O'.

When I was old enough to catch the school bus with my brother, I would share part of my packed lunch with O. It never occurred to me to feed him the food I didn't want to eat. We were buddies. Again, my brother would tittle-tattle on me when we arrived home.

"*Mum,*" Jude called out to assure Mum's full attention, "I think you need to put a timer lock on Gabi's lunch box. She's sharing her food with O while we wait for the bus."

He was expecting Mum to react and scold. "I think it's lovely. I'm proud Gabi loves animals and is willing to share. It shows she has a soft heart. A lot of young kids find sharing exceedingly difficult." She winked at me and then touched Jude gently on both shoulders as she smiled into his eyes.

"Do you remember when you were her age, and the animal farm came to school? I'll never forget," Mum shared dreamily. "As soon as those cute fluffy yellow chicks were released, out of all the kids sitting in the circle, they made their way straight to you. One even nuzzled under the open flap of your anorak."

From then on Jude and I both shared our lunches with O, although Jude was more circumspect about what he offered.

As I grew older, my brother would still, at times, take the opportunity to exert his first-born, only-son prominence over me. Aged seven, I wondered whether O was a boy or girl. Jude surreptitiously googled on his phone to appear the all-knowing one. I was savvy enough to know the 'smartarse' in my brother but would never say so.

"They're all girls. Males don't have a penis," he announced, impressed by his own ingenuity. And, as if he hadn't impressed enough, "They *love* anting!" His phone was firmly back in his pocket. He'd obviously found an article, 'Ten Strange Things You Didn't Know About Crows'.

I fell into the trap. "What's anting?"

"Gee, you don't know much, do you! They crush ants and rub them over their body like perfume."

"Does it smell nice?" I queried innocently.

Jude raised his eyebrows and sighed. "No dumb-arse, it's formic acid. I wish I had some – it keeps pests away." He looked pointedly at me.

Mum overheard and exiled Jude to his room. Later he would be made to apologise sincerely and with eye contact. Mum also hit him where it hurt, not between his legs as I would have, but through his pocket. The consequence for calling me a dumb arse was ten dollars. Five dollars for a derogatory word and five for including a body part.

Ultimately, my bond with O deepened with the birdbath and bird feeder platform Mum bought. I made a daily ritual of filling the birdbath with fresh water, and on the platform I put unshelled peanuts.

I discovered over time that, while crows are exceedingly generous to those they consider genuinely benevolent, they hold grudges for those they remember as enemies.

From my connection with O, I became an avid collector of the beautiful. My childhood collection included each precious item O gifted me. He would clear the feeder of peanuts and sporadically leave a shiny tribute to our friendship on the empty tray. I kept everything in a large plastic container with a snap lid and compartments. Inside were rows of small objects in clear, plastic bags. I had written on each bag with a permanent marker, the day, date and time of each gift - *silver bell, Jan 2012, 2:25 p.m.* Over the years, he gifted me paperclips, Lego pieces, single earrings, a hinge, part of a broken light bulb and a small piece of ocean-tumbled amber glass.

As each piece arrived, I would take them in for news at school. My teacher was more indulgent of my passion than my classmates.

"Not again," grumbled Dylan Turner, "I'm bored with crow stuff."

I found such a comment rather hypocritical. Dylan was always bringing in insects, worms, fish, small mammals and frogs - all delicacies to crows. I think Dylan was jealous of my passion and, as a hands-on kid, he took it badly each time I would reveal my latest treasure with the introduction, "You may take a close look but please don't touch".

Dylan would be on O's hit list. As my best friend, O certainly would retaliate on my behalf by dive-bombing him to and from school. Birds of a feather stick together and never forget. Even in high school, I was never fond of Dylan Turner.

After I feed O today and coo with him, I recall two pieces in my childhood collection. My second favourite was a pearl-coloured heart. I still remember saying to Mum with great joy, "He is showing me how much he loves me." My brother had rolled his eyes but kept his mouth zippered. By far my most precious gift was a tiny flat piece of shiny metal shaped like half a heart. Across one side the edge was lightning bolt jagged. Engraved on it were two words. *Best For.* Still to this day I like to think O had the other half secreted away in a safe place. *Best Friends Forever.*

◯ THE WATCHER

Every morning a crow comes and sits at my window. He never enters through the door as do all the other customers. Always, he settles himself outside as a still silhouette central to the only window along the length of the cafe's frontage – a window showcasing the civic heart of the CBD and a pedestrian mall.

Morning outlines in the near and far distance, a square flanked by designer shops and expansive sandstone buildings. A solitary busker plays his violin. The dulcet tones of Vivaldi's *The Four Seasons* soften the day. Little in the way of crisp wafered brownness places this as an autumn day.

A black-clad figure of solitude, Crow is one of our regulars. He sits nestled precariously amongst the round-backed wicker chairs, his broad shoulders sloping downward. Surprisingly, despite his tall, solid build, he perches with both nonchalance and comfort. To my sensibilities, only the vertical world of the sandstone pillars of the old Federation bank building to the left match his physical presence. A haze of greying hair scarfs his neck between the fingered-shiny edge of his black trilby and the collar of his coat. The centre curve between the twin peaks of his hat mirrors the distant shape of pigeons freed from the earth-bound constraints of sandstone and concrete as they glide, rise and dip across the jigsaw-piece sky between the buildings on either side.

Crow's needs contrast starkly with the yuppie city set who, to the hidden disdain of smiling baristas, turn ordering a coffee into a foray into fine dining. He sips his Belgian hot chocolate (all he ever orders) with mastery, finely balancing his sipping rate with retention of heat till the last drop.

It is when he embraces his mug with both hands that tenderness for this stranger fills me. Their once fineness and competency are marred by a slight tremor and beginning gnarls of arthritis. Despite betraying his situation in life, the black fraying edges of his tailored coat sleeves are powerless to lessen the overall elegance of his appearance.

As winged creatures coo and wait, he saves the two small biscuits, wrapping them in a serviette. I know he does not take them home, as he never puts them in his pocket as he leaves.

His mug is still warm to the touch when I clear his table.

We never speak beyond the morning's pleasantries. He invites neither acknowledgement nor conversation, as his spirit appears to be on a journey that requires no companion. Perhaps it's a kink in his soul – a shyness that only allows solitude's trickle. I only ever hear him mutter, "Good morning" as I bring his usual and a, "Goodbye" as he alights from his perch with a doff of his trilby.

Of all the customers, he intrigues me the most. I wonder about his who, what, why, where and how. I sense the answers would hold a magnificence beyond the greyness of the ordinary.

As watcher my observations are all I can offer. It is your turn to finish this story. His story. I have laid word crumbs for you to follow. Imagine what you will.

I am listening.

In the beginning, there was a six-year-old boy ...

✑ WITHIN ORDINARY DAYS

Agatha Milton was at the age when women become invisible, but it did not stop her from presenting as a waterfall of warmth even as her days stretched into sameness. It was a Thursday afternoon in April, and she was cashier on the '15 items or less' checkout. It sure beat the conveyor belt checkouts where she'd heard customers complain to one another in the queue about the Marvel Heroes Super Discs promotion. Spend twenty dollars, receive one disc – forty-two in all.

"I've spent $3,200 on groceries at this store and still not found '42. The Hulk' to complete my son's collection. So much for the 'Collect Them All' slogan. It was supposed to be fun but it's so expensive, exhausting *and frustrating*. My son's *so* disappointed."

Agatha listened as she packed. What was it with today's parents and kids? Desperate, exhausted and disappointed with a piece of plastic; a mix of entitlement and unnecessary wants in a whirling world. She'd even heard Pass the Parcel had morphed into a gift for every child. Exposure to small disappointments – valuable training for youngsters.

Then there was today and every subsequent Thursday at three-thirty, when Agatha noticed the boy and his mother. Her basket was full of the thirty to sixty percent specials for the week and never totalled more than forty dollars. Agatha suspected she did the bulk of her food shopping at Aldi.

"How are you today, love?" asked Agatha, ensuring her eyes were not engaged with her hands as she spoke.

"Okay," replied the woman, who behind her brown eyes had a look of, *I don't know if I'll be able to pay the rent this week,* rather than, *I'm done with you, Woolies. My son can't complete his collection.*

"How's your little fella doing with the discs?"

"We keep on trying. We're only looking for the one. The Hulk."

The woman shielded her lips with her hands and whispered, "He turns eight in June … bought the keyring-lanyard … keeping the discs for his birthday."

"Well, good luck, love. I hope you find it."

Agatha handed the woman one disc and then turned to the boy. "Here, love, you put these aside for your birthday." She winked at his mum. "I put these aside, they're the discs certain customers don't want with their purchase. You know the OINKS, DINKIES and SINCS."

The woman looked confused.

"One Income, No Kids. Dual Income, No Kiddies. Single Income, Nine Cats."

The woman smiled and, for the length of time it takes a camera shutter to open and close, her face lost its weariness. The woman looked thoughtful, then replied, "Guess I must be a SMOK – Single Mother, One Kid."

Thus, a weekly ritual developed between the three of them. For Agatha it was a pure delight when the boy shared with her how many discs he had, including the extras she gave him, and how he and his mum had made a cardboard box for them.

Mid-April became late May and the promotion finished.

On the first Thursday in June at three-thirty in the afternoon, Agatha was on duty at the self-serve checkouts when she spotted the boy and his mother outside the store. Agatha saw him approach. It was a delicate happening. As he handed her a homemade cupcake with chocolate icing and multi-coloured sprinkles, she noticed the lanyard around his neck – '42. The Hulk'.

"That's incredible. Hulk's a rare one. I'm calling you Mister Marvellous from now on. Happy birthday. Thank you for the cupcake."

The boy ran back to his mother who waved at Agatha, and then put her palms together, her fingers level with her chin, and mouthed, "Thank you."

Early June turned to August and then to Christmas in September.

Agatha had only just begun her fifteen-minute rest pause at work when young Sam windstormed in with an, "*OMG. Really!*"

"What's wrong, Sam?"

"Early-onset diabetes from stacking the mince pies, shortbreads, puddings, fruitcakes, gingerbread men and candy canes."

"I know, Sam. They are stacking all the magic out of Christmas."

"And Easter. I'll be out there with chocolate eggs as soon as the Christmas decorations are down at home."

"Hey, Sam, mentioning Christmas, you were stacking stubby holders yesterday. I've taken a photo of one on my phone. Notice anything?"

Sam looked at it. It fitted the bill. Neoprene and standard fit for a 375ml can. He'd prefer the patterned triangles of trees to be tones of green instead of blue. He turned his attention to the large white circle announcing a red *Merry Christhmas*. His brow furrowed and he bit his bottom lip. It didn't look right, but he wasn't sure why. Something in the middle?

"Look, Ag, I'm not the best person to ask. I'm decent with a 2B pencil and acrylics, but I suck at spelling."

She read it out to him.

"I reckon it's ironic – a few beers, and I slur my words with the best of them."

"A pedantic customer's sure to spot it, Sam."

"If it's a typo I guess it'll be a case of stack 'em up, take 'em down. I'm having a coffee. Usual for you? Peppermint tea?"

"Make it coffee for two."

"Well, that's a first, Ag."

"Seem to need a little boost lately to keep me going."

Sam drank and scrolled his phone. Agatha was happy to sit in silence. Next time she'd ask him about the progress of his HSC major artwork – a custom-spray recycled surfboard with the title, *Tails of the Sea*.

Agatha rose, slowly and reluctantly, from her seat. Lately, constantly tired, everything seemed an effort. Perhaps at sixty-three, the four-day roster, Monday to Thursday and every second Saturday, was too demanding. She'd negotiate with management if her oomph didn't return. Thank goodness she wasn't working tomorrow.

As she walked back to the register, she spotted Mister Marvellous and his mother well past their shopping time. The boy ran to Agatha

in his floppy way, something behind his back. As soon as she saw the
stubby holder, she knew what he was going to say.

"Well, Mister Marvellous, do you know you're the first customer
to spot the mistake? I bet you're a whizz at finding *Where's Wally?*"

He ran back to his mum and turned to look at Agatha before he
disappeared round the corner. His smile expressed it all.

When she saw them again, towards the end of a late shift, Agatha
found out why she never saw them at three-thirty anymore.

"Liam and I are doing a paper run. Advertising material. We
do it after school. Tell Agatha what we are saving for," and she
turned to him.

"For a bike for me for Christmas."

"Wonderful." Poor little tyke, she thought to herself. A weekly run
pays about twenty dollars, and even a bike at K-Mart is about two
hundred. Tight deadline. His mum would put it on lay-by for sure.

Agatha was relieved when her shift ended. Ten p.m. Her feet
were aching and burning from the standing. Within five minutes of
turning the key in her front door, she did what she'd never done before.
She went to bed in her clothes, teeth unbrushed, face unwashed.

She was asleep in thirty seconds.

A side sleeper, she had over the past few months taken to lying
on her back, her left breast increasingly tender and itchy. She'd
changed her washing powder to sensitive and disciplined herself not
to dismember the garden waste with the long-handled secateurs all in
one go. The fourth option was … well, she was too exhausted to think.

The morning was into double digits when she stirred. As she
took off her clothes her left bra cup stuck to her nipple. *Ouch!* She
stood under the shower till the patch softened. As she patted herself
dry, a sticky pink discharge oozed from the left nipple. Suddenly,
fatigue morphed into *fear*. It bullied her into alertness with a panic
that coursed through her chest and throat – a toxic pairing of fright
and flight.

Four days later, Agatha and a mammogram with bright white specks and irregular clusters and a core needle biopsy result waited for the surgical oncologist to speak.

Agatha heard the letters 'DCIS', but her mind wandered … DCI Banks, British crime drama series. Banks, a no-frills Yorkshire cop. Like him, she'd draw on the extraordinary within her ordinary. Great series …

"Mrs Milton … Mrs Mil—"

"Oh … sorry, Professor Mender, I seem to disappear into a world of my own lately. Please repeat what you were saying."

"You have DCIS, ductal carcinoma in situ. This means the abnormal cells are contained and haven't spread to the breast tissue."

"*Oh, thank goodness.* Does that mean I don't need a mastectomy?"

"Yes. The surgical margins are clean. We'll only need to remove the clusters with a lumpectomy. When the scar's healed, it will be barely visible. You'll be pleased to know the results are hormone receptor-negative. You won't need hormone therapy."

Agatha's eyes slid from his eyes to his hands. They were the delicate, sensitive hands of an embroiderer, or a creator of a thousand origami paper cranes.

"My receptionist has the paperwork and will book you in. Any questions?"

"Recovery?"

"You'll be in one or two days. Back to work in three. Then there will be a three-week break if you decide to go ahead with radiotherapy."

"Radiotherapy. I was hoping to avoid that." She knew the potency of the beams. Left side too, next to the heart. "How many treatments?"

"Normally it's a protocol of five days a week for three weeks, the choice of an afternoon or morning slot. Most people experience fatigue, especially at the midpoint. Radiotherapy's proven to lower the incidence of recurrence by fifty to sixty percent. The radio oncologist will provide more precise information when you see her. Ensure you lock in dates and times before surgery."

A fundamentally unfair proposition – damned if she did and equally as damned if she didn't. Thank god she'd accumulated enough sick leave to cover her time off. She didn't know how people managed to work, look after young kids and cope with the fatigue of radiotherapy. She remembered her beloved Reg. A trifecta of chemo, a radical cystectomy and radiation for bladder cancer with no winner, and a handicap of blood clots, pain and near suffocation. If he'd survived, she'd be a grandmother by now.

On her last shift before surgery, she told Sam she'd be off work and why.

"Oh, Agatha, I am so sorry."

Coming from Sam, who turned whatever he could to one syllable, she knew how sorry he was. What happened next she didn't expect.

"You know what, you're one lucky woman, Agatha Milton. This week, after twelve months, I am now no longer on my learner's licence. I'm indelible-inking myself in to take you to your radio-therapy sessions. I've already arranged for my shifts for three weeks to be from seven to midnight."

"You knew?"

"Only yesterday. You know how things get around in a workplace. Glad I knew, as it wasn't such a shock the second time, and it let me arrange things ahead."

Agatha was too stunned to speak – she gasped. She and Sam only exchanged general chit-chat when their rest breaks aligned at work. Other than that, they were strangers to one another. She remembered reading somewhere, it's the least expected person who'll be a friend indeed – expected others, missing in inaction.

"Oh, Sam, what can I say except thank you from the bottom of my heart. You're a kind young man. One of life's blessings." *Sam,*

God love him, all sun-bleached hair, sun-and-salt-kissed skin and a laidback manner.

"You've my mum to thank. She brought me up with six words of advice: be kind, be kind, be kind."

The surgery and recovery were excellent. The friend missing in action? Well, the one who never checked how she was until she wanted to borrow money. Agatha's closest friend had dropped her off for the surgery, collected her, filled the prescriptions she needed and bought takeaway for them to share.

Sam arrived at Agatha's home for her first session with Hello Kitty slippers with silver sequined uppers and faux fur trims. "I thought these would come in handy. Radiotherapy rooms are like the frozen food section at Woolies."

"How come you know that?"

"Dad got cancer when I was fifteen. He's fine now."

"Sorry you all had to go through that, Sam. Glad he's well now."

"Thanks, Agatha. Got everything?"

She nodded and pushed something into his hand. "Don't you dare say no, Sam. I don't want you out of pocket with the petrol."

"You're so thoughtful. Thank you, Agatha."

He held the car door open for her and off they went.

The visits felt like an excursion and, even on grey days, his gentle humour and measured chit-chat eased her heated heart.

Tattooed coordinates the size of discreet pinheads of graphite marked the spots for the irradiated beams. Agatha felt vulnerable each time she lay on the table. Bare-breasted, with her arms in stirrups above her head, Minerva's disc of strategic warfare and medicine hovered whirred and buzzed above her like an alien spaceship. One pass over her, one withdrawal to the left, a beamed close-up shot, then the retreat and Agatha's release as the table slid forward. Released till tomorrow but not from the thought of the potency of Minerva's jaws

– forty times more than a regular x-ray. How she *hated* that machine. Bliss was she realised, the space between surgery and radiation.

Days became increasingly like the one today when she'd needed to fill a prescription at the chemist in the small set of shops at the end of her street. No energy to walk. No energy to drive. No energy to make a cuppa. Then … then … the raw peeling skin around her aureole.

Sunday, eleven in the morning and Agatha was still in her pyjamas. Next week, the last week. Despite only three radiotherapy sessions remaining, internally the whole of Agatha cried out wanting to be heard. *Enough is enough. Leave me be.* All the fight irradiated out of her, for the first time in her life, Agatha felt brought to her knees. No reserves to continue.

Her doorbell rang.

Agatha trudged limply to the door. *Sam.* She hoisted a smile.

"Sorry to disturb you on the weekend. I know you need to rest, but I think this is important. The manager gave me this for you. A customer dropped it in at the cigarette counter."

"No, that's fine. Come in. Take a seat."

As she opened the envelope and card, a green disc fell into her lap. In a large-spaced uneven childish hand, she read:

Sorry, you are sick. Hulk is the strongest one there is.

I hope he makes you strong and okay again. BY Liam. XX

"Ag, you're crying. Bad news?"

"No, just heartening news and exhaustion."

She handed Sam the card and the disc.

"I'd love to hear the backstory if you're up for it, Ag."

"Sure, Sam. How about coffee for two and, while you're here, I'm offering you your first commission. In November, when your HSC is over. It involves this disc, a custom-spray and a bike helmet."

✍ VALLEY OF THE SHADOW

(i)

It was the thud of sudden impact. She was amazed the kitchen window hadn't shattered. Her first thought was the neighbour's son with a tennis ball. Opening the sliding door to the timber deck and garden, she scanned for culprits. There were none. Her eyes sniffer-dog downward, she searched out the yellow roundness that the redness of the timber decking would betray. Puzzled at not having her assumption met, she saw it.

A Pre-Raphaelite green like the first unfurling of spring. Light. Small. Elegant. No larger than the length of her hand from fingertip to wrist. Its head jerked on a still body. Her heart wanted this delicate creature of the blue freedom to be stunned, her head told her it was otherwise. Within moments the head jerks ceased and all was silent stiffness.

She picked the bird up and laid it in her palm – such a perfect fit. She stroked its warm breastbone and soft feathers and took in its open eyes. It was the death of a bird for which she had no name. It was no noisy mynah, no willy wagtail, no laughing kookaburra. It was a bird of fineness and greenery with a dove-like head and beak.

A few turns with the trowel into the dark rich freshly-rained-on soil was all it took to bury it. The whole incident upset her deeply. How quickly death comes, when life is in full flight, fooled by the illusory reflection of foliage and sky.

Bird.

Breeze.

Foliage.

Flight.

Solid Air.

Solid Surface.

Falling numbness.

Open-eyed, paralysed panic.

Death by confusion.

(ii)

It was a fine morning, though clouds were bunching to the west and there was a keen edge to the breeze.

It was a perfect day to die.

The old man had had enough. Enough of the walls, the lying there, the innocent taunting of the expanse of blue sky and the isolation of hearing, but not partaking in, life beyond the windowsill alongside his bed.

His daughter noticed the necrosis of the dying in his Dachau-like body. Withered muscle, flesh hung like soft elephant hide and his blue-grey eyes clouded, cataract-like.

One morning he caught her off guard with the matter-of-fact statement, "I'm bored."

The day before the old man had been confused and apprehensive. He felt he was going insane. "There are clocks along the picture rail. They're all showing a different time. Too many for me to fix."

"Morphine mirages," the daughter reassured him.

He settled.

By nightfall he was an immobilised automaton with only the breeze of a breath.

Hours passed.

The daughter took his hand, stroked and kissed his forehead and whispered tenderly, "It's time to let go, Dad." And she left him.

At eleven p.m. with one rasp, he died.

As the nurse re-dressed the old man's body, the daughter stroked his feet. She noticed how rapidly the cold and stiffness set in, how quickly the fingertips faded to pale blue.

Five years from vigour to frailty and now this, the carapace.

The daughter wept for what would never be again – his presence, the seeing and hearing of him, his touch, his energy.

The old man met death on his terms, fine-tuning it as he had clocks and cars. Left it till the last minute but not late enough to inconvenience anyone. Friday, 22nd December.

Do widzenia, Tatus.

Goodbye, Father.

Zofia adapted to the daily rhythm of her grief till the tsunami softened to a ripple. It was only then her father came to her. It was a delicate happening, and it pleased her.

He came to her in her son's elongated earlobes, the curled edges of his lips when he smiled, in his innate charisma and quick wit that drew people to him, his energy and his passion for cars and motorbikes.

He came to her in her daughter's aliveness in cold weather, her natural ease and hunger for the eastern European lifestyle, in her Slavic looks and her perfect accentuation when she learnt Polish.

Her father was there even twenty years later when her daughter decided to study at the Jagiellonian University in Krakow and obtained Polish citizenship, and when her son inked the harp of his ribcage with the Polish eagle.

Zofia learnt that the lost and the loved are found in the living.

On an identical fine morning, where clouds were bunching to the west, and there was a keen edge to the breeze, it was a perfect day to remember.

Czesc, Tatus.

Hello, Father.

You are with me – always.

(iii)

Death called on Veronica Claire Hanlon with the stealth of a squatter who wanted to take physical possession without consent and without detection.

In an October beginning, there was a small marble-sized lump. Then the MRI: *Attention! Please discuss these results with your medical practitioner. The terminology contained in the enclosed medical report may easily be misinterpreted.*

Fair enough.

She opened the over-sized clinically-white envelope and examined the images; tributaries flowed to a white mass like water into a lake. This picture did not paint a thousand words. It painted one. A nine-letter word … malignant.

Left breast, six centimetres, at three o'clock.

Biopsy: HER2 breast cancer, stage two.

HER2, an arrogant marauder with radical ways: malevolent trickster; aggressive, wanton profligate; immortal, libidinous bloodsucker. Choiceless and at the mercy of the merciless, her healthy cells were for the turning.

The feeling of dread was absent. No dry tight mouth, no quickness of breath, no panic. It was confirmation of all Veronica suspected – something was life-threateningly wrong.

The lump and the dragging fatigue happened as a genetic switch untouched for twenty-seven years clicked from off to on; cell division to support a growing foetus mistimed to post-menopause.

Her treatment of annihilation? A trifecta of barbaric protocols: poison, slash and burn. Three sacrificial altars of healing. Chemotherapy. Surgery. Radiation. In Veronica Hanlon's war, there would be collateral damage.

December was docetaxel (the medical equivalent of RoundUp) to shrink the tumour before the slash. As predicted by a fellow veteran, when she washed her hair on the tenth day its thinned filaments clung like cobwebs to her face and hands. She had two thoughts consecutively.

It has come.

I am not having this.

Veronica Hanlon became the Red Queen. *Off with her … hair!* Shaved, she was triumphant, empowered.

"You're amazing, Roni," her closest girlfriend Jenni declared, "you carry on regardless. No fuss. No falling apart. Knowing you as well as I do, I suspected you wouldn't. Sassy under fire. That's who you are."

"Look, I sympathise with women who are traumatised by the loss of their hair. For some it's their crowning glory, but my hair had little going for it besides its gloss and straightness. In the words of a gay hairdresser I went to once, 'Your hair's got no guts.' What is there not to like freed from haircuts, root touch-ups and bad hair days?"

Mind you, Veronica Claire Hanlon voiced this before the hair vanished from her armpits (never to grow back – a bonus), her eyebrows (thank god for cosmetic tattooing) and then – her fanny. She loathed her pre-pubescent fanny. It didn't go with her facial wrinkles and the slack hillock of her belly. When she looked in the mirror, she knew not to ask who was the fairest of them all. It was beyond doubt she had all the sex appeal of Gollum. Like Gollum, corrupted trying to protect her precious – life from death by stealth. She wanted her adversary annihilated.

She uttered it before a four-year-old playing at the ocean's edge blurted, "That lady looks like an alien." His mother distracted him, hoping she hadn't heard. True, thought Veronica, but his raw honesty filled her with the sadness of an outsider in desperate need of a kindness beyond Panadol Rapid and Endone for her bone and muscle pain.

She declared it before she had coffee with a friend in a small up-market shopping plaza and an affluent woman approached her with, "Excuse me, my son wants to know why you're bald."

WTF. Veronica thought the woman should have ordered a slice of emotional intelligence on the side when she'd ordered a babycino and half-strength soy latte, extra hot, to go. Looking at the child, Veronica was gently forthright, "I am sick. I take medicine to make me better, but it makes my hair fall out. It will grow back." She did not remember if the woman wished her well. All she remembered was that the woman left with the smile of the oblivious and the self-congratulatory.

Then came other docetaxel-induced adverse events. The time of the reddening, the browning and the withering. Small bright-red lesions on her face, chest and back. Her toenails browned. The nerves in her feet damaged, and her feet wooden and burning like feet on sun-hot concrete in synthetic-soled shoes. Veronica Claire Hanlon, the hairless, limping leper.

Amazing seeped out of her like the intravenous infusion. Drip by drip. Hour by hour. Week by week. Month by month. This thing. What it demanded was relentless. She struggled to find the woman who had looked back at her in October. She hid the horror and her repugnance beneath a base coat and two applications of red nail polish, but all she saw was the brownness hiding beneath the deceitful veneer of red. Shame surged like polluted water on a savage king tide pounding her resilience, tumbling and tearing her soul until, with the falling tide, who she had become shivered and lay like tresses of uprooted seaweed along a sandpaper shoreline.

A first-place winner. A hard-won victory. The tumour shrank. A lumpectomy would retain her breasted equilibrium but with less volume on the left. It was a hallelujah moment, but she only had the energy to say, "I should bloody well think so. I'd be incredibly distressed if it hadn't worked."

March sliced through her breast and delivered a second-place winner. The surgeon's hands cut and stitched with seamstress precision, leaving a scar from the spoils of war no lover would notice – ultra-fine, plumbline neat and with time, healed to imperceptibility.

Then the bliss of a four-week reprieve between surgery and radiation. Her hair grew back as salt-and-pepper sproutings. She ran her fingers over her head. "Feel this," she murmured to her son and daughter, "I'm a velvet hedgehog." Since childhood she'd been fond both of velvet and Mrs Tiggy-Winkle. She felt a gentle joy, a connection akin to seeing the first colourful hello of blossom on a plant when the weather warms spring to life.

April triggered four permanent pinhead tattooed coordinates, like blackheads, on her cleavage and inner left breast. The Minerva system of targeted radiotherapy. Thirty treatments. Six days for five weeks. On the home run. Collateral damage? Fatigue, tears and a red raw, peeling aureole.

June came with the sharp slap of winter and relief. The aggressive marauder was dead. Two weeks after surgery, to ensure it did not regroup, bind and duplicate, there were three hundred and sixty-five days of targeted biological therapy. Eighteen cycles, three-weekly of intravenously infused Herceptin. Cruelly sweet – possible heart failure. Fortunately, her ECGs remained stable. Christmas came early for Veronica. November. Her treatment at an end.

In remission, she retired two years early and redefined what was important: to live in the now – no past regrets, no future fears – and to take the path of least resistance.

For her it was not, as some survivors' claim, the best thing that had ever happened to her, but for now, Veronica Claire Hanlon had won her war.

IN THE MIRROR

ℰ WHAT?

Hate it when people ask, "What do you do?" Best to reply, "When?"

They'll reply, "What do you mean, *when?*"

Repeat yourself. "When?"

With bewildered frustration they'll respond with, "*You're a bloody idiot.*"

To which I reply, "Look, mate. At the moment I'm relaxing having a beer. When I visit the travel agent later, I'll be a customer. For the whole of March, I'll be a tourist."

This is met with another, "*Bloody idiot!*" and defeated withdrawal.

As a car concierge at one of the city's top hotels, "What car do you drive?" is another question never to ask me.

Ask me, "How?"

You'll find me a pussycat.

ℰ DIAMONDS ARE ...

"I really love your diamond necklace ... can I have it when you die?"

Her mother didn't take offence, after all her daughter was only twelve years old, and Irene wasn't planning to die anytime soon.

At nineteen, her daughter had asked the same of her engagement ring. Her mother upgraded her response to a Medusa stare.

At twenty-nine and now a woman of glitz and glamour, her daughter had a $19,000 diamond engagement ring and a future husband Irene disliked. Now fifty-three, Irene admired the ring and said to her daughter, "Tina, darling, your ring is stunning … can I have it when you divorce?"

THE BOOKSHELF

Whilst it is not suitable for applying lipstick, a bookshelf is a mirror. So, let me introduce you to Nina's reflection.

A room with large and small, read and unread books soldiered along the length of hip height downlit alcoves that line two walls. Clusters of diversity: personal development, guilty pleasures, escapes, memories.

Care of the Soul, Thomas Moore.

The Great Philosophers, Stephen Law.

How to Win Friends and Influence People, Dale Carnegie.

Shoegasm: An Explosion of Cutting Edge Shoe Design, Clare Anthony.

The Cancer Recovery Guide, Professor Kerryn Phelps.

Book of Longing, Leonard Cohen.

WHO AM I?

As innocuous as I appear, those of my kind balanced effortlessly between the thumb and forefinger of bold emperors and tragic starlets.

Impermanency has smudged us all.

Proud cedar forests were felled for me and the earth cracked open.

The physical abrasions of metallic grey upon the white that I leave for posterity can so easily be erased until all that is left is a paper tombstone of snail-tracked indentations.

With each repeated sharpening, wood and mineral against steel, I face mortality.

Always, always ... the cocoon of the razor-edged, steely tomb until, mere stump, destiny dictates I become either a schoolboy's prized possession of the miniature or am speared into the depths of the paper bin. A world of

the fractured,

the unwanted,

the pulverised,

the crumpled.

When my end and point meet, I wish only for a flight into silken softness.

⟨❦⟩ A LIFE INADEQUATE

The Philips Azur Elite iron needed to blow off steam. "I'm fed up to my water level with servitude."

To emphasise its point, it glided across the ironing board, angled its soleplate towards her and let out a burst of turbo steam.

"It's your purpose," Eleanor protested.

At this, Azur Elite let out a violent burst of searing steam. "How *dare you*! I was never given any choice in the matter. *Look at me!* My body is a work of art – a sculpture." And it plummeted over the edge of the board, dangled by the cord and swung.

Eleanor placed it back on the board with a reproving look. *Trust an iron to be exceedingly dramatic – always able to go from cool to hot in the flick of a dial.* "Okay, okay. Tell me more."

The Azur Elite angled itself for full appreciation of its sleek, elegant profile. "I need a life of leisure. I want others to admire my beauty."

Eleanor stared at the iron, admitted to herself it was an iron with the lines of a Chevrolet Corvette sports car, and promptly cut off the cord. Where was she to put it?

After a tour of the house, she placed Azur in one of the alcoves alongside her other smaller sculptures in the living room.

To decommission Azur was an easy decision. At 2.2 kilos it was too heavy for her arthritic hands. Hands whose right index finger proceeded to order a Phoenix Gold Free Flight – cordless, non-drip on low heat and a mere 0.8 kilos.

⟨❦⟩ ELIMINATION

She only wanted five minutes. Five minutes to sit on the toilet and bask in the satisfying feeling of solitude and letting go, *but no!* Young children are like stalkers.

"Go away!"

It came out in a voice both alien (not hers) and recognisable (her mother's).

Something inside her recoiled, slug-like. Then came the note.

Mum is meen to me evin you I am so soft do you know
what I meen I am so sad.

Instantaneously, she wrenched the recognisable taproot upwards out of its nourishing unexamined darkness to wither and die like a weed on hot concrete.

⌾ AMAZING GRACE

In the Garden of Paradise

Beneath the Tree of Knowledge,

Bloomed a rose bush.

Here, in the first rose, a bird was born.

'The Phoenix Bird', Hans Christian Anderson

It is frequently from the embers our dreams arise, and it is the playful symbolism of our subconscious that illuminates our souls and from whose depths our true selves are revealed.

Prologue – The child

She sought out the photo album that captured her childhood in black and white. There it was. A monochrome photo of a girl aged about five. The girl has fine straight dark hair in a bob. Her simple dress shows smocking across the chest. The girl is neither pretty nor plain but has a face that interests. She is unsmiling. Her eyes look beyond the camera at a distant space of her own knowing. Her front teeth lightly nip her lower lip. Even from a cursory glance, it is evident this child's existence is not carefree. In her look is worry and concern – a search for answers to questions a young child should not need to ask.

The child as a young woman

"Tell me about the dream you had the night before," prompts her therapist.

Her dream is still chromatically vivid as her dreams always are – a nocturnal theatre of images whose symbolism always reveals hidden truths daylight disallows.

"I was in my dream. I'm a young child. I sit beside a coal fire with my elder sister who is seven years older. She is close, but away from me, and to my right. We do not speak. We are in the room that forms part of the middle level of our home, sandwiched as it is between our living area below and the bedrooms at the top. It's an unfamiliar room kept solely for the rare entertaining our parents did and for piano practice. A room permeated with unfamiliarity where invisible menace and malevolence lurked. I still feel its oppressive air and the nightmares this part of the house gave me. As a child it was a wasteland, unwelcoming and cheerless. I never told my mother how I felt. She'd certainly and impatiently dismiss my impressions as childish imaginings."

She pauses and laughs nervously. "I feel embarrassed to admit it now ... piano practice was a terrifying ordeal. Always, I checked behind curtains and chairs sure goblins and witches lurked there ready to do me harm when I wasn't looking. God, it's no wonder I never took to the piano." She laughs lightly, and her therapist smiles. "Now, where was I? Oh, yes. As my sister and I sit by the fire, I'm warmed and mesmerised by its steady heat and gentle crackling melody. Suddenly, a small sparrow flies into the flames. I expect my sister to rescue it, but it is as if her presence dims as the bird reaches the flames. Fear, horror and a deep sadness overcome me. I cannot bear to see it maimed or devoured by what warmed and comforted me in the cold of my surroundings. Then, miraculously that tiny darling bird flies out as unscathed and unconcerned as when it flew in. My dream ended there."

"Why a sparrow?"

"As a child sparrow were constant in our garden. So small. So happy-go-lucky. They comforted and reassured me on a deep level. Made me feel safe in the world."

Her therapist considers all this for a moment. "It's a powerful dream. What does it mean to you? I want the first thought that comes to you."

No need to think. She already knows what the whole dream signifies. "The bird is me, the child – small, defenceless, insignificant. I survived the trial by fire of my childhood. I've come far from a place that could have scarred me for life. There's the saying, 'What doesn't destroy you, makes you strong', but it's more than that. It left my essential core untouched. The fierce heat didn't vitrify my gentleness, my capacity to care for others and to love, although it formed a protective shield around it for a time."

"What enabled you to survive and eventually flourish?"

"My own ability for learning and growth. I've wisdom, will and courage. I was always making things as a child and spent hours alone. In creation I sought, and found, beauty, balance, comfort and a sense of myself in the world. When I made things, they absorbed me, time stopped. What I created held me within it, and I held it within me. Even now I feel my most content and whole when I'm creating."

Yes, she says to herself after the session, *how well I've survived and eventually flourished. If we are lucky, our deepest wounds become our greatest strength.*

She no longer feels the remnants of the old deep sadness that wept within her. The grief over never having the mother she needed. Home had been a lonely unsafe place lacking the soft expression of love a child understands – no warming home fires. Instead, destructive flames fuelled by a frustrated, vitriolic mother and a physically-present but emotionally-absent father. She lays no blame at their feet. We all possess a history to overcome or succumb to.

The young woman as a mother

It is evening and, as she lies in bed reading, her thoughts turn to her daughter, aged ten. Her mother and father are long dead. She reaches over the side of the bed and opens the bottom drawer of the bedside table. The drawer is full of mementoes and loving secrets. Tied in a translucent wide ribbon with silver polka dots is a pile of all the cards and notes her daughter has written to her over the years since kindergarten – thirty in total. Each one as much her daughter as the day she wrote them. Loving expressions.

> *Merry Christmas, to my most loving mother.*
> *My present to you is my heart! I hope you will love me forever and ever.*

There is also a child's magical world and a polite request for a heartfelt need to be met.

> *Dear tooth fairy, I know this may sound a bit selfish, but I was wondering if I could have my teeth back because I miss them.*

There is one, a reprimand, when fatigued and overstretched she had spoken harshly to her daughter.

> *Mum is mean to me. Even you. I am so soft. Do you know what I mean? I am so sad.*

Her daughter becomes a teenager, and between them is a closeness that lays to rest the past and heals generational wounding. In this, the mother feels such strength and joy. She knows the secrets of her daughter's soul and would never destroy its precious wholeness and beauty. Still, as a mature woman, she wonders what perversity, unhappiness or lack of will had made her mother cruel. It was as if her own mother chose only to see her own shadow side in her daughter.

Her rage meant she had never been able to see her daughter for who she truly was.

How different we are as mothers, she muses.

She sees her own daughter as a precious child entrusted to her guardianship – to nurture, to delight in her triumphs and to comfort and support her in her trials. To cultivate not to crush. To watch in awe as the tight bud of childhood unfolds to yield the soft full blossom of womanhood. Support. Protect. Enhance.

Epilogue – mother and daughter

It is evening, and I watch this darling girl of mine, Grace, with wonder, awe and love as she silhouettes against the gold and crimson of the setting sun. 'Red sky at night, shepherds' delight.' There is contentment and peace in my heart. There is no need of fires tonight nor for cinnamon, spikenard and myrrh for the air is sweet with the aromatic spiciness of star jasmine and the intoxicating perfume of port wine magnolia. She comes towards me, this child of mine, hugs me and calls me 'Mother of Life' as she frequently does and, as her eyelashes flutter against my cheeks, the air smells doubly sweet.

> In Paradise
>
> When thou wert born in the first roses
>
> Beneath the Tree of Knowledge,
>
> Thou receives a kiss,
>
> And thy right name was given thee.
>
> 'The Phoenix Bird', Hans Christian Anderson

✐ APOCALYPSE-FREE MORNING

A blend of fact and fiction, this story is based on a Reddit thread about impulsive responses to imminent death by burning. The responses range from the banal to the outlandish. Names are fictitious.

Hawaii – Emergency Alert: Saturday, January 13, 2018 at 8:00 a.m.

Incoming Ballistic *Missile Alert* sent via Emergency Alert System and Commercial Mobile Alert System over TV, radio and cell phones.

Seek immediate shelter.

This is not a drill.

Notification of False Alert: Saturday, 13 January, 2018 at 8:30 a.m.

Sam Atkins decided to leave no carbs behind, so he ate all the leftover lasagne in his fridge.

When told by her family of the alert, the ninety-five-year-old matriarch stated, "Pop the kettle on for a coffee. The power will be out soon." On the all-clear, she demanded pancakes with the lot.

Jason Steele longed to bring out his best brandy, smoke an expensive cigar and do trails of coke off a stripper. Unfortunately, he was stuck roadside with a flat tyre and no spare.

The couple eating at Café 100 in Hilo realised that on an island there was no place to go and, goddammit, they'd already paid for their meal.

Jackson Kalina filled his emergency water containers right behind his garaged car. Trapped by one hundred and fifty gallons of water would mean an awkward call to work.

Smiley and his mate watching college football on TV together were decidedly apathetic towards death. They took pride in remaining cool dudes under all circumstances. However, Smiley did become drunk after four years of sobriety. *Oops!*

Sherri Stevens's first thought was, *Shit, I'm going to die a virgin.* She grabbed her flatmate. "Time for die-soon-sex. Forget the condom." The encounter led to a nuke baby they named Duke.

James Dougherty called his wife to tell her he loved her and to apologise for his part in their recent fight. The threat of turning into a burning crater led him to develop the theory of 'nuclear therapy' – random missile alerts do help people put their shit into perspective.

A firefighter from Honolulu began duty ten minutes before the missile alert. His first thought was, *Fuck me! Why does shit always happen on my shift!*

Always the practical joker, Dan Osborne thought it would be kinda ironic to microwave a packet of popcorn, even perhaps stuff his orifices with unpopped corn kernels. His gravestone? *Here lies Sweet Corn Osbourne.*

Tim Morrison cracked open a beer, went outside to his garden and got ready to watch the show.

Louisa Jamieson felt nothing but sudden silent shock and became a Christian for thirty-eight minutes. Sally Winters in the apartment opposite found bliss in ignorance. She slept right through.

Dougie Walters a young marine woke his mate with, "There's a missile incoming."

His mate replied, "They'll shoot it down," and turned over and went back to sleep.

Elsie Lansdowne in Oahu cleared out her fridge and with her cell phone battery at two percent entombed herself. Apart from the five hours and twenty-two minutes of unnecessary incarceration, her only regret was that she hadn't taken the tub of Baskin-Robbins triple choc fudge ice cream in with her.

Seventy-year-old Arthur Cunnings ate two cans of baked beans as he hid in the closet.

He later regretted it. Noxious fumes are never pleasant.

Jane Gruntle a tourist from Australia was as mad as a cut snake because the hotel had no nuclear shelter. She rated her stay on TripAdvisor one-star (the buffet breakfast had been adequate) and she vowed never to stay there again – the hotel or Hawaii.

All survivalists went to their underground bunkers.

They are expected to resurface in forty years.

So,

Think, what would you do?

Cool, calm and collected?

Adrenaline-fuelled?

Unaffected or dejected?

Yes, please tell me do, what would you do for your final adieu?

꧁ LOST IN NEW ROME

Police Interpreter's Transcript

A public nuisance? Yes. As they say back home, I was *confusie e obstinate.* Hey, those police who bundled me into their car drove in true Roma style – red lights ignored, siren full blast. Look, the only excuse for my behaviour is this. It was my very first flight. I watched the in-flight movie *Sleepless in Seattle.* But for me, I was *Stubborn in Queens.*

My nephew told me everyone loses forty-two minutes to traffic jams each day. "Avoid arriving at rush hour when the congestion load is at seventy-four per cent."

"Sure," and I booked an early arrival flight and just packed hand luggage.

The flight to Rome? *Fantastico!* Only five hours. However, I was upset and disappointed my nephew wasn't there to meet me as planned. *Grazie a Dio.* I had his address, but how things had changed since I left Italy when I was nineteen to live with family in Mexico City. *Parca vacca!* So modern. The ancient city's landmarks? Gone. Adding insult to injury, and to my growing anger, all I heard were American accents. Everywhere. *Porca miseria!* Even the street signs were all in English. *Sacrilegio!*

Luckily, I met a fellow Romano – the policeman directing the traffic. I cannot tell you the joy in my heart and ears to speak to someone with the same dialect as me. *Bellisimo!* I asked for directions to the bus station. He gave me excellent instructions, but twelve hours later I was no closer to my nephew's home.

My apologies, I forgot to mention, I speak little English. Frustrated, tired and hungry, I returned to the airport. I went up to the first uniformed person I saw – *another American accent!* Like a red rag to a bull. I was lost, and all he did was bellow at me, "*New York. New York! NEW YORK!*"

Then, the euro dropped.

I calmed. Finally, I understood. *Col cavolo!* I'd disembarked from the plane at the refuelling stop at JFK Airport.

Rome?

Another nine hours.

ℭ REDEMPTION

The true story of 'Painting the Town Red'.

Henry Beresford was born with a silver spoon in his mouth, lord and earl at thirteen and 3rd Marquess of Waterford at fifteen. All this privilege at an early age had made the worst of him come out of the woodwork. His devil-may-care attitude was over the top, and he was known for his eat, drink and be merry. It is pulling no punches to say he was a rotten egg and was regarded by many as a lost cause.

For his friends, the lunatic fringe, life with Henry never had a dull moment. *Carpe diem* was their call to arms, and making mischief became a force of habit: wenching, overturning applecarts and throwing bricks like hot potatoes through windows. Their mindlessness when drunk was unfettered. The most civic spirit Henry ever showed was at Eton when he stole the headmaster's whipping block. All in all, he was too much.

At twenty-six, after a day at the races, he and his friends went on a bender in Melton Mowbray. Alcoholised into action in the wee hours of April the sixth, Henry and his cohorts vandalised enough to cause a Vandal's toes to curl.

On reaching the city tollgate, Henry saw red when asked for the required fee for the tollkeeper to open the gate. Repairs had been underway on the gate, and there were ladders, buckets and pots of red paint. Without fear or favour, the tollkeeper finished up a ruddy mess as did the constable who intervened. Adding insult to injury, Henry nailed the tollhouse door shut and painted it red too. Then, onto the town knocking over flowerpots and wrenching knockers off doors. Doorways were reddened, and the Old Swan inn sign swung from white to red. Miffed that the Red Lion required no repaint, into the canal it went. As young muscles flexed, the turbulence continued. As police arrived in their bobby blues, they departed bobby beetroot.

Two years later, by a stroke of luck, Henry hung up his boots, called it a day and waved good riddance to his mischief and mayhem. Love had made him come to his senses.

He fell head over heels, happy as a lark, walking on sunshine, stars in his eyes in love with pretty as a picture, virtuous Louisa Stuart, a lord's daughter. It was a *coup de foudre* – love at first sight.

For Louisa to consider this bull in a china shop as a suitable suitor, her father thought she needed her head examined.

"Bear in mind he is crazy about me and aims to please. I've set my heart on him and as for an engagement, the sooner the better."

"Be that as it may, I know only too well he has shown himself to be a scoundrel. To this, I cannot turn a blind eye. It is a stumbling block to my consent."

Henry fretted for the first time in his life. Had he shot himself in the foot with his smack-dab smashing past? Had it come back to bite him?

"Sir, you've three years to prove yourself. The forever straight and narrow for you, sir, or there's fat chance of you ever taking my daughter's hand in marriage. *That* is my line in the sand."

Henry set about treating his tenants more humanely and even helped the worst affected in the Irish Famine. After three years, Louisa and Henry were still over the moon with one another and tied the knot.

He and Louisa had twenty beautiful years in seventh heaven until Henry broke his neck in a riding accident. Louisa was shattered as was Henry, and she never re-married. He had been the love of her life, and she had been his.

RAINMAN

Bill Buckley searched the paddocks for a four-leaf clover – *all bloody threes*. The situation required an extreme measure. Plan B. Dance naked under a new moon. It'd better bloody work. The land was as dry as a dead dingo's donga.

As a three-year-old, his mother had allowed him to pee outdoors when it rained heavily. Wild and free. Strewth, decades had passed since he'd felt like that. Farming was hard yakka.

Maybe it was the allure of his expansive flesh, as his feet thundered on the tessellated earth, that lured the brown snake to attack rather than slither off. Thank god he'd worn his sporran with his mobile inside.

Siren blaring, the local ambulance arrived driven by his son-in-law. It'd be all around town by evening. Bill didn't care. He had neither dignity nor reputation to uphold. It was open knowledge in the township he was as mad as a cut snake. His mates were sure to take the piss.

What he did care about, despite the pain, was the sound of rain on a white aluminium roof. He pictured the ambulance's windscreen wipers hyperventilating from left to right. *Stone the crows. You ripper!*

Recovered, his first trip to the boozer went as expected.

"Welcome back, Rainman. A Nude Vodka Soda on us, mate. Just watch out for them snakes."

☞ THE CHALLENGES OF LEN GRADY

The Fort

Len, at six was the youngest of three children. His older brother by nine years and his sister by four were always telling him he was a nuisance. The song 'Santa Claus is Coming to Town' confused him. Lists of who's naughty and nice, who's been bad or good but not the word 'nuisance'. Where did that leave him? On the list or not? The song did mention 'don't cry or pout', and he knew he did a lot of both.

At six, he knew a fair bit about Baby Jesus – he was born in a land with lots of holes, was nice and would never cry or pout. He felt sorry for Jesus. He only got three presents: gold, Franky Scents (which Len assumed was an aftershave like the one his dad used) and smurr. He thought Jesus would have preferred a toy castle and chocolates. Kings did not know what boys' want, not like Santa.

Len was, however, not sure where Jesus was born except it was a long way from Tyneside. He also wasn't sure why his brother and sister had smirked and rolled their eyes when he responded to their question of what he thought the shepherds had brought. Len agonised for a few seconds and then asked hesitantly, "Wez it a pie?"

More worrying to Len was the incident that happened after the second day of opening the flaps on his Advent calendar. Noticing his lack of interest in opening it, his mother discovered he had eaten all the chocolate squares (naughty but nice) and closed the flaps neatly back to hide his deed (bad not good). His father had been furious, but his mum was accepting. "Look, love, lads will be lads, especially our Len." It was the only thing that rescued him from a good hiding. Still, Len thought, Santa would surely not leave him off the list.

In bed on Christmas Eve, Len's agitation grew. What on earth was going on down there? He heard hammering. Didn't his father know reindeer were sensitive to loud noises? Len silently cried himself to sleep knowing reindeer would never land on the roof with such a din going on.

In the morning Len's eyes lit up. There under the tree was the most incredible wooden castle complete with functional drawbridge and four bastions on the corners with their tops painted bright blue. His favourite colour. Santa has also been thoughtful enough to leave a packet of plastic knights with horses, catapults and ladders.

The paint on the castle was still tacky. Len realised he had scraped onto the list at the last minute. There and then he decided he wasn't going to sail close to the wind next year. He gave away pouting and ill-gotten chocolate and commenced helping his mum with the dishes to which his mum would say, "Whey aye, Len, that's so canny of yee. Yee are such a good lad."

Yes. He would be on the list next year.

Seven Years Later … The Cake

The home economics class was making Christmas cakes. Most of the boys were using round tins. Not Len. His was square. The teacher allowed him plenty of leeway as he was the quickest and most thorough at cleaning the countertops at the end of the lesson. He also impressed her as, unlike the other boys, he knew a teaspoon from a tablespoon and that twenty drops were one ml.

"Yee canae dee that!" Eric shouted.

Len said, "Calm doon," but his eyes said, "Get lost ya wazzock."

"Miiisss … Len's nicked me marzipan!"

As the other boys concentrated on fancy piping in red and green, along one edge of Len's cake a sloping mound of marzipan waited to be iced.

"Aalreet Len, what's that?"

"Propa ski slope, Miss," and he pulled out of his pocket one plastic skier and several fir trees.

All the boys applauded and laughed.

Knowing his best friend well, Tommy added, "That's our Len fer yee, Miss, isna it?"

Yes, Lee got away with murder as well as marzipan.

Twenty-one Years On … The Prank

At times like these Cheryl wished she'd thought twice, ten years ago, about saying, "Aye, I dee" to the question, "D'ye tyck this man, Leonard Stanley Grady, te be yer laaful wedded husband?"

At nineteen, he'd charmed her with his confident fun-loving ways and wooed her with his natural charm, his creative competency with a range of power tools and his ability to bake a pavlova. Never one to conform, his free-range antics had now in a grown man become ridiculous, an embarrassment. This latest was one deception-for-a-laugh too far.

"It wez just a lark. Ah bet ah'd get a free meal, and they reckoned ah couldna. Wi wez aal drunk, an' ne-one wez agyen it. They reckoned me plan were pure belta. Canae a guy dee what he likes on a Thursday neet oot wi the lads? Yee waad not hev known if Tommy didnae open his gob 'cos he thowt youae'd find it funny. Stop blatherin' on aboot it."

"Na way, if yee dee an aaful thing, embarrassing yorsel an me, as yer wife it's me job to caal yee on it."

"Youae got te be oot of yer mind. It wez only eight cans of Stella. Wea're talkin' twelve pounds."

She'd tried the, "When yee … Ah feel … What ahneed yee te dee is …"

It failed to work. No surprise there. Len did as he pleased.

Tommy had told her how Len covered the cost of the extra eight cans he never had by ordering a samosa at £3.25 and a lamb laziz main at £8.75. He asked Adhish, when they were all about to pay the bill, for the eight cans he'd put aside in the restaurant fridge. Embarrassed, flustered and unable to find them, Adhish waived the cost of Len's meal.

A dose of his own medicine is what her Len needed to force him to think outside himself. At thirty-three he needed to take a seat at the grown-up table. She'd appeal to his joy of the absurd in a matter-of-fact, deadpan way.

The next day he came home from work and casually asked, "Myek a cup of tea wud yee, pet."

She did.

She filled a cup with hot water, dropped a yellow plastic letter T into it and placed it gently on the table in front of him, "There yee go, love."

He looked at the cup and, as quick as he was, he responded calmly with, "I'ave changed me mind. A'll heva coffee instead." He'd scupper her. No one, especially not his wife, got one over on Len Grady.

This time she filled another cup from the kettle, placed it in front of him, made a cough and added an "Eeee."

He pushed his chair back across the tiled floor with his left leg and rose with an exasperated, *"Alreet!"* He pulled fifteen pounds from his wallet and threw it on the table. "If it's so important to yee, yee go and see ta it."

"Sorry, love. Not happenin. It's na me who's accountable fer the asshole-y trick yee played when yee were out fer a blowout with the lads."

"Ia've had enough. Get off me back will yee. Ahm off te the boozah."

He stormed out of the kitchen, and by the time he returned at eleven-thirty the bedroom light switched off in unison with the turning of his key in the front door.

Bedtime was silence and backs.

In the morning he opened the fridge door to find his head in a jar of green liquid.

"What the hell is this, woman?"

"Read the label, Len."

She'd labelled the jar *Pickled Idiot* because that is what he was at the time she'd taken the photo at his work's Christmas party. He'd fallen flat on his back on the dance floor doing the YMCA, nearly taking a string of people with him.

"Look, yee can keep this up, but yee knaa me, ita'll change nothin. Yee might as well not dee tha. Leave it alone, woman."

She did.

For a day.

On Sunday morning at six o'clock, daylight was pushing through the dark, and the air from the open window had an enlivening edge to it. A perfect morning for golf. Cheryl was still dozing, blinded by a satin eye mask embroidered with *Disturb At Your Own Risk*. Sundays were her lie-in morning. Len padded down the wooden stairs to the kitchen. The fridge had no unwelcome surprises. No face looked out at him from the bottle of milk. The packet of Weetabix was unopened. Perfect. She'd let it go.

At six-thirty Cheryl heard the garage door open and Len's Nissan Juke drive away. He'd be out at least four hours, five if he had a quick beer with the lads afterwards in the clubhouse. Her husband was a Cadbury drinker after golf – a standout storyteller over a pint-and-a half.

At ten-thirty she took a spare car key from the hallway drawer and drove her Mini Hatch to the golf course, parking out of sight of the fairway. She walked to his car, opened the door and lowered the driver's window until it was fully down. She sprinkled three millimetres of honeycombed shards of tempered glass on the ground outside below the door, placed a heavy hammer nearby, then tucked takeaway menu from Adhish's Bangladeshi Restaurant under the driver's side windscreen wiper. She then lay down on the back seat out of sight. For the final touch, she rang her friend Cynthia who worked on reception at the club and asked her to announce over the club speakers, "Waad the owner of car registration NE60 SMR please return te heir vehicle immediately."

Perfect timing.

Len was finishing his last few mouthfuls of lager. "See yee lads."

In the car park, as he approached his car and skimmed past the bonnet, he noticed the leaflet on the windscreen and initially thought it was an infringement notice.

"What the …"

Simultaneously, Len connected the printed paper with the shards.

"The firkin bastard … tha will cost me … Ah well hev him fer tha."

Len turned away from the car as, in full fury, his clammy index finger unsuccessfully prodded the fingerprint ID button on his iPhone. He turned ready to hurl the phone at the car, only to see Cheryl appear like a jack-in-a-box in the driver's seat and to hear a word he was all too familiar with saying but not receiving – *"Pranked."*

Enraged and gobsmacked, one part of his brain took a few seconds to settle until the other half was able to connect what had happened.

"Fer god sake, woman, yee are leik a terrier wi a bone."

For a moment, she thought she'd gone too far.

"Ah gis up. Ia'll put it right. Ia'll caal in on the way hyem an' apologise. Say ah made a mistake."

She got out of the car with a dustpan and brush and a plastic bag.

"Yee sure did ... hold this bag will yee ... Ahm glad you 'ave come te yer senses. I wouldna want yee setting a bairn of ours a bad example. Ah want our laddie to look up to his fatha."

He looked at her, "Dyer mean ... "

"Ah dee mean, Mister Leonard Stanley Grady."

He gathered her in his arms and swung her around.

"How dyer knaa itae's a boy?"

Cheryl mentioned nothing about a sudden craving for salt and spice or about her increased availability over the past four months for sex at six in the morning. What she did say was, "A mutha's intuition."

That night as Len spooned her in bed, she hoped he'd modify his attention-seeking ways and become a father his son would be proud of.

As Len drifted off to sleep, he mused about the devoted father he would be – from bump to birth to boyhood and beyond. He also wondered about one other vital thing. Where he could buy an extra-large t-shirt printed with *One Pint*, and a size zero with *Half Pint*.

THURSDAY

8:35 On waking you decide to do your pelvic floor exercises followed by tai chi. Two thirds of the way through – arch, hollow, arch, neutral, stop wind, stop wee, pelvic floor on, core on – mobile rings.

8:46 Daughter. Flight details you need to lock-in and book immediately.

9:01 You ring Virgin ... waiting ... waiting ... need to poo. Still waiting. You place your mobile on the bathroom window ledge alongside the first sample vial from the bowel testing kit and paper for the toilet bowl. You're now sitting on the toilet with your back to the whole kit and kaboodle. Forget the kit. The pressure's on to finish the poo before you're through to someone. You're pulling up your panties when two things happen simultaneously. The you-are-on-hold music stops and the front doorbell rings. What the ...! Quick decision. Take call, ignore doorbell, postpone flush, lid down.

9:17 Flights booked. Phew! Flush. Wash hands. Sanitise mobile. Open the front door, package waiting. Ah yes! You remember – *Inside Japan* brochure. November, autumn travel. Back to exercise routine.

9:47 Mobile rings again. Car dealership. Servicing complete. Driver *may* be on his way to pick you up. What? *Maybe?* Can't contact him. He has a hearing aid, and his phone will be off. Explains his irregular speech intonation from the drop-off yesterday. Only ten minutes away. Still in your pyjamas. Rush to bathroom. Quick shower. Dress. Face cream. Lipstick. No show. Back to tai chi. Get as far as *white crane spreads its wings* ... mobile again.

10:08 Driver not on his way. You figured that. He's left to go to the post office. What would suit as pick-up? After his morning tea. 10:40. Great! Finish tai chi – energised, relaxed. You think how certain days are monasteries and others the stock exchange. In-between would be perfect. You drink your morning alkalizer – apple cider vinegar, fresh ginger, turmeric and warm, filtered water. Mobile, yet again.

10:21 Close friend catch-up chat. Now it's your stomach. It's bashfully whispering it needs food. You're listening, but you and it know it will be a twenty-minute wait after you sip the last of your muddy lip-pursing brew.

10:35 Sipping through a stainless-steel straw, you forward the Virgin emails to your daughter. You are still writing all this. Thoughts wander. Your mother said, as a baby you took your bottle so hot tears coursed your cheeks. Familial myth or fact? Choice or adaptation? Mother whose inner forearm was heat insensitive? Doesn't matter. The tepid is always a turn off for you – food, drink or relationships.

What a beautiful cover the brochure has. White background on quality card with three cascading koi from top to bottom along the bound left-hand side. Largest in the foreground, smallest at the top edge. Illusion the koi are swimming towards you. They form a graceful arc of infinity. The koi in the foreground with grey rings circling the green of its iris looks as if it's had a late night. Middle koi has a goitre issue. The smallest, side-on, is Cyclops-like. The four hues of blue from turquoise to lapis combined with apple-green surrounded by fine-drawn grey ripples place the koi fluidly on the cover. White space is the reverse magician here. It draws you fully into seeing what is there. Your observation and active mind only cease during orgasm. Then you are all sensation and primal sound.

Time to put the pen down. Finish the one-third of your drink. You flick the pages of the brochure. You think how each one is worthy of professional framing. You feel warmth infusing your heart space. The ginger? No. It's the rising call of adventure. The day is quiet. Time to delve beneath the surface of the day. Buddhist temples, southern islands of world-class art, hot springs, volcanic sand baths, geisha and sumo, countryside cycling, shogun castles, temple rock gardens, traditional ryokan accommodation.

10:56 Doorbell rings – driver from the dealership. Gather and dash. Mental list: buy supplements from health shop; peruse two op shops and pop-up jewellery stand in the shopping centre; eat brunch; call-in at the travel agent. Library – return and borrow.

14:13 Home. The opaque afternoon sky asks nothing of you. The delicate rain on the green and brown soothes. It kisses the pond sparkler-like. It is a lullaby. You do your meditation.

6:24 You finish typing this story. It's only your second attempt at second-person narrative. Or is it stream of consciousness? Perhaps a hybrid. Always, the unexplored beckons and you courageously and inquisitively follow. You like that about yourself.

LOSING UNA

As the prison gate closed behind him, he saw someone he recognised.
I knew she only gave in because she was lonely. Only child. Single. Motherless and the wrong side of forty. I recognised her as you do someone with whom you are familiar. You sense it, know by sight their walk, their posture. Seconds before the gate closed, I turned. As I turned, I caught the moment. The moment her stiff stillness became the staccato click-clack of heels on the concrete fading to snow-cold silence. The moment her black-and-white judgement won out over the redemptive synergy of forgiveness and memory.

I had drained her mother of colour – a pillow against her face. A face that no longer recognised those she loved. A mind that could not hold onto the present, the past a loop of successive takes. There was no rain that night and, above the stilled silence, a full moon. I blurted out on the phone, "Your mother is dead." Numb muteness, and then her tears as I stonewalled my heart in silent static misery and longed for the unrecoverable.

For my act of loving violence, at sixty-four, I am lost to the world for ten years – perhaps to my daughter forever. I must wait and hope.

Trust that she will forgive me for having loved so deeply and always said, and shown, too little.

Amongst her mother's possessions she found ...
I am angry. Alone. I cry myself to sleep. *All this because of you!* I hate myself for missing you when all I want is the freedom of indifference. I hate you for leaving me to sort out my mother's possessions, forcing me to remember what I try so hard to forget. *Hate you. Hate you.* Hate you for the problem of the box to which *you* have the key.

A writing lap travel box of flame mahogany, inlaid brassware and joints dovetailed to patient perfection. You made it for Mother for an anniversary, and we gave it to her together over breakfast. I was six at the time. In the night I was woken by soft music and, as I reached the bottom of the stairs, there you were dancing with my mother. As a child, I felt safe and loved when your large hands lifted and hugged me, but that night I noticed something else as your hands held the small of Mother's back and her silky shoulder, something beyond a child's understanding. I understand it now – intimacy and tenderness.

I stare at the box. It beckons, *open me ... you know you must.* It's the must I walked away from yesterday. *You* have the key. I need to know what is inside.

Reluctantly he handed over the key.
Lockets. Diaries. Letters. These are private affairs, and I am a very private man. The request for the key is typewritten. It arrives the day after my daughter chose to turn around and walk away. The signature is Times New Roman twelve-point as if ink, like blood, is too personal a marker. I relent. What she will find can only do good where I appear to have harmed.

Since I requested the key, I'm still sorting through my mother's things. I pause for a break and look out of the bedroom window. It's early afternoon. A dull day uncertain whether it is sun or cloud.

The doubtful sky reveals slices of sunlight as it peek-a-boos with the clouds.

The doorbell rings. I rush from the back of the house to the front and unlock the door, but no one's there. I look downward, and propped against the terracotta plant pot is a small Express Post padded bag. I know what's inside. I'll open it tomorrow.

After breakfast the next day, I open the box expecting to find a diary, papers and a bundle of letters. Instead, I discover only three things.

The first sits atop an envelope as if freshly taken off. It's my mother's large Victorian black enamel locket and 18ct gold belcher chain. Inlaid gold swirls of delicate trailing stems and leaves edge the heart. In the centre, a 𝑈 – Una. She wore the locket always. It encircled her slender neck just short of the valley between her breasts. I slip it off the chain, place it in the palm of my right hand and roof my fingers over it enclosing it like a precious pearl inside an oyster shell. I close my eyes. Slowly, the heat of my hand warms the enamel. I see my mother's svelte body, delicate features and bobbed straight black hair and hazel eyes. Never vanilla, she was an emerald green and buttercup-yellow woman with a magical ability to draw others to her.

I open my hand and then the locket. On the left, my father as a young man looks out at me: blonde hair that dips into a widow's peak and deep-set, heavy-lidded, brown eyes, high cheekbones and full lips. My father's pensive default face became joyous when he smiled and laughed. His calm depths allowed my mother's melody to glisten. Others were drawn to him because his quiet assuredness aroused curiosity. Everyone listened when he spoke.

On the right, I see me as a girl, solemn and unsmiling. *How I hated being photographed.* I have my mother's hair and my father's eyes. I close the locket, place it back in the box and pick up the envelope. I recognise its bespoke white linen paper and its red silk lining. My father's paper of choice.

14th February 1980

Happy anniversary, my darling!

I knew when I first saw you, that you were the one for me.

We have been married ten years and still, every time I put my arms around you, I feel that I am home. I know you experience the same because when my hands stroke your back and you nuzzle into me, you shiver, and I see the goosebumps rise on your bare arms.

Such tenderness I feel for you and a passion hidden from everyone but us. I am yours forever, my darling friend, companion and lover.

We both know life can be unpredictable and fragile. Please remember, in sickness and in health, you will always be precious to me. At such times, I will be your rock. There is nothing I will not do to protect you and our darling daughter.

Your adoring husband,

Peter. xx

How he cherished her. How at times I felt overlooked. An outsider. A welcome visitor in a home marked by two. My father, our protector. Is this what this is all about? Is his mute acceptance of the prison sentence penance for what he did? Is it about exiling himself from a life that has no meaning beyond her? Am I so angry because he felt I needed shielding from the progression of my mother's disease? I have no answers.

The final item is a beige fabric pouch like an oversized spectacle case. It has two pockets with zippers. I open the smaller lower pocket to find it contains two AA batteries and an ear receiver. I open the top zipper, shake the pouch and out slides a silver Sony IC recorder the size of a chunky KitKat – the locked-away answers to my questions. My instinct tells me that whatever it contains, it's not going to be easy listening. I put everything back in the pouch and leave it on the coffee table for another day.

My night in bed is full of wakefulness and dreams, both invaded by an electrical current of fear that courses through my body, between my breasts and nibbles at my fingers. Relentless, it does not stop. Saturated with anxiety and exhaustion I surrender, and I am it. Still, it refuses to leave.

When morning comes I lie in till eleven, my eyes masked against the sunlight. After a strong coffee and a light breakfast, I play the first message. It is fifteen minutes and fifty-six seconds long. My father has recorded it in high definition. I hear the piano – Beethoven's 'Moonlight Sonata'.

The first movement enraptures with its slow, steady, quiet tempo and sombre rolling triplets that sway back and forth. The fleeting melody's light glistens through the dark notes. I see my mother's right hand and her pinkie finger cutting through the accompaniment.

The second movement where the notes run up and down the keyboard is too light and flowery for my taste. It is as Liszt said, 'the flower between two chasms'. It is the third and final movement – dark, roaring, fluid, powerful and passionate – that holds me captive and breathless with its intense, unbridled, intricate rhythms and speed.

Emotionally exhausted from listening, I pause the recorder. My eyes linger on the wall filled with framed memories of a family intact. Now, I see only the gaps of bare wall between the photos as missing pieces of a jigsaw puzzle that spite has swallowed. My mother a songbird on the wing who flew over the fields unminding of the barbed wire fences below became tangled in what life held beyond the melodies and beautiful harmonies.

I need to eat or rest. I stop the recording unit and lie down to listen to a guided meditation on my iPhone. I hear the instructions (breath through your belly, then your chest, your abdomen), and then I am out. I wake up three hours later. It's four p.m. I am morose and groggy, having heard nothing of the app but the beginning but knowing why I am angry with them and angry with myself. Thoughts turn and tumble like balls in a tombola.

My father and my mother did what they did without including me. I supported my father from a distance, but I should have done more. It always seemed what was between them had space for only two. Ends always have beginnings.

In the beginning were the mild anomalies in my mother's behaviour: forgetting where she'd placed something for safekeeping; names that were once fluent on her tongue stalled or forgotten for a moment; an inability to focus on a task without her mind and actions diverted onto another track; her recall of events and conversations shaky; the banana skin in the top loader instead of the bin, until their multitude became the aberration that is Alzheimer's.

I noticed on my last visit, before my overseas transfer, how she found it increasingly difficult to follow conversations. During dinner she'd listen intently, a blank expression behind her eyes. She was lost. When she ceased to follow, she would interject with an off-topic much repeated amusing anecdote from her past. I'd say, 'Mother, you've told us this before' but she'd continue regardless, determined to be included. My mother now the outsider and between my father and me, the unspoken but the known. I always knew to say a 'yes' if she offered me a cup of tea; otherwise, she'd continue to ask because her memory needed a visual cue.

I stay in my pyjamas all day. All I want to do is cocoon.

At eight p.m. I curl up with a hot water bottle pressed against my chest not because it's cold, but because I need to feel it's comforting warmth. At two a.m. I'm awake. I make a hot chocolate and sip as I listen to another recording. I skip to one mid-way on the unit. It begins with my father's voice.

"You play so beautifully, you always do. I can listen to you for hours."

Then my mother, an aware moment. "Peter, darling, I feel afraid. I'm lost. Something's missing. My heart knows it, and it creeps up on me like a dread … How long do we have?"

"Before you forget again?"

"Yes."

"Yesterday it was for five minutes."

"Days like this I'd rather be ignorant of my forgetfulness. I am a prisoner tortured by my emotions of fear, dread and panic." Then, her voice urgent and anxious, "Please, please, when I cease to exist, help me go. I know I can trust you to know when the time is right. Promise me that, Peter. I don't want to be palliated."

"My poor darling, I promise. For now, together, we will live in the present moment. Come what may, you will always exist for me." My father's voice is potent, calm and reassuring. "Here, let me sit behind you. Lean back against me so I can circle my arms around you. Let me warm your hands in mine. Close your eyes, feel our breath in rhythm, listen to my voice. Say after me – I am safe. I am loved."

She echoes it three times. She's suddenly calmed, diverted. "I'm so hungry."

"Come on. It's time for lunch. You know how you love egg, mayo and lettuce sandwiches with the crusts cut off. Let's go out and see if those good-for-protein pets of ours have laid any eggs." I hear the patio door open and then my mother's voice, "But it's snowing!" I hear my father laugh. "Una, it does look like snow. But it's spring, and it's the blossom from the pear tree. Look, see the bees? I know, I'll collect the eggs, and you can pick some flowers."

"*Look at me, Peter.* I'm swimming in sunshine. I'm so happy. I'm going to hug you."

In the silence that follows is, until he has control of his words, the space before tears when the cheeks warm and pressure builds up in the back of the throat. My father's voice quavers, "I love you, Una."

"I love you too. We love each other very much … hold my hand. I don't want to get lost in the park."

"I'll make sure you get home safely. We have eggs and flowers to take home, remember."

Awareness. Oblivion. A faulty power switch of reappear and disappear and the shrivelling in-between the two. All of it here. *How dare it rest so lightly in the palm of my hand?*

When my mother plateaued and then, within months, faltered, fell and disappeared beneath the waters of Lethe (the underworld river of forgetfulness), I recall her Lilliputian tributes to the beauty and freedom of the outdoors. I never knew my mother owned so many little vases. Raw compassion rose in my chest, intermingled with fear. Always she was a woman of the flamboyant, the intoxicating. A woman of the lily, gardenia and her favourite, night-scented jessamine because its botanical name sounded like a title for a piano composition – Cestrum nocturnum.

Now, she was smaller, flatter – a wallflower.

"How long has she been doing this with all the vases?" I asked my father at the time.

"It's just started. It gives your mother pleasure to wander freely in the garden now she doesn't have the autonomy to leave the house on her own anymore. You know how much beauty and independence meant to her."

"And the incontinence pads?"

"You found one?"

"I wondered what the smell in the wardrobe was when I went to hang up her dress from the dry-cleaners. She'd popped one into the pocket of a jacket."

"Poor darling, she's embarrassed. She's always hiding them. I just find them and get rid of them."

I bring myself back to the present. My need is not for my memories but for those entombed in the unit, the truth of the middling years of my mother's disease. I start the recording again. My father is beginning to lose her.

"Who are you?"

"I'm your husband Peter. That's you and me and Kate on the DVD we're watching. Do you know who Kate is?"

My mother stalls, "I'm trying to remember … do I know her?"

"She's our daughter, Una."

"What's the matter with me?"

It's the core question throughout the recordings she asks regularly like a short-repeated phrase in music.

To entertain my mother and to stop them degrading, my father digitised all the old film reels from the 1950s and the videotapes from the seventies. When my mother heard the transferred sound from the high-end Super 8 movie reels my father took in the mid-sixties, she'd squeal with delight, her hands clapping like an excited five-year-old. Other times they distressed her as did the mirrors. My father removed every mirror in the house after she began to slap her reflection repeatedly and ask, "What are you doing here?" Her unremembering frightened and confronted her and, like a bully, taunted her with her shortcomings. At these times I marvelled how creative my father was with a box of high-quality art prints. He kept the images simple. They looked at them together and made up a story. I was a part of it once. A part of the remarkable, the magical. He'd fan out a few of the A5 prints like playing cards from a deck. "Choose one for us, Una … It's Banksy's *Girl with Balloon*. She looks happy to me. What do you think, Una?"

"Of course, she's happy. She adores the wind in her hair and on her skin."

"She must like red too," I add.

"Yes, red is a happy colour. The little girl let the balloon go because she's sending it on the wind so that everyone who sees it will feel happy."

My father strokes my mother's hands gently. "I agree with you, Una."

"Me too," I say. "Look, the girl's feet are together. That means she's letting the balloon go. We could send a balloon of our own in the air."

"Yes, yes … *now*. I want to send lots of balloons in all different colours."

"We'll all go for a walk, buy the balloons, and Kate and I will blow them up."

My mother never turned down an invitation to go out; it's the only now of the before.

The girl and her red balloon – all I can see is a story of loss without hope. Like my mother, the balloon floats away to lie in some foreign place, deflated and less-than.

Gradually I stopped visiting as frequently and, the truth is, I hoped I didn't need to visit. It was a two-hour drive each way. I used the fact she no longer recognised me to justify my absence. If she cannot remember me, then surely, I cannot be missed. I avoided the joy I felt those times she remembered my name when I walked through the door, and I avoided the tearing grief when, in my eagerness to catch her with a hug, she'd slipped beyond me, unable to reciprocate. That day, I left with a mantra in my head. Do not look back, walk away *as fast as you can*. Shame surges and quavers in my chest with the raw acknowledgement I not only thought this, I acted upon it.

I restart the recording. The middle folders are conversations between the two of them: halting, dreamy and repetitive minutiae of caring freighted with unspeakable pain. A vase becomes a cup, a comb a toothbrush. I check the dates. The recording is a record of plateaus that drop further into the abyss every three or four months till the tsunami of forgetfulness leaves her nowhere to drop. My darling father responds to the repetitive minutiae as if he has heard them afresh. Lost to herself, he allows her to remind herself of who she was. As a furniture restorer, my father was a haven and refuge for fragments – restoring wholeness, radiance and beauty to the damaged and the broken. A man whose grace and goodness under fire my mother never took for dullness. A man who took responsibility for his own life and the decisions he made – unlike his father, a feckless charmer whose throw of the dice dispensed a wife and discarded a son.

I skip to the two recordings near the end – the thief of who, what and where has come bringing silent stillness.

"Aren't you playing today, Una, darling?"

"Do I do that?"

"Yes, you do." Silence … "Here. I'll put your fingers where you need to start."

Suddenly, instead of fingers stroking keys, I hear a sound as unexpected as tropical rain that pelts against windowpanes and demands to break and enter. But this, this is the sound of my mother's hands hitting her head and bare skin in a terrifying clapping tempo that increases in ferocity. "No! … No! … *Stop.*" It is my father as I've never heard him before: an imperious voice full of angst. His voice morphs into soothing slowness, "You'll hurt yourself. I'm going to hold onto you very gently. That's right. You just rest your head on my shoulder. I'll stroke your hair. You like that." They are united in the ocean of their salted misery: his of loss and longing and hers of forgetfulness. Then he begins to sing softly to her, 'That's Amoré', but I sense his deep sorrow mired within its swaying rhythm. *Enough!* Without memory, there is no music. *That's enough for me today.* I am beginning to fill in the gaps in my mother's deterioration since I left three years ago. Tomorrow I will skip to the last few recordings.

Despite a nine-hour sleep, I greet the new day exhausted. Another day to face, when all I want is yesterdays long gone. I don't know if I can listen to much more of a past life and the small deaths within her, but I steel myself and switch the recording unit on. Classical FM plays in the background and above it is the slow intermittent scrape of a spoon on the edge of a bowl. "Just another mouthful of porridge. You look like an adorable baby bird stretching its neck out waiting eagerly for the next mouthful. You must be starving." Fifteen minutes later, "Well done, my darling. All gone."

"Who am I?"

"You're my wife."

"*No, I'm not.* I'm your sister. You're Roland. On my seventh birthday you gave me a ballerina music box. It played 'Für Elise' ... You said its tempo suited me. Remember?"

With its simple harmonies and a light-hearted melody, it became the first piece of music my mother learnt to play on the piano.

My father knows the story well, and he slips readily into his role in her reality. "Yes, I remember, Una. I said it was graceful and gliding like you, but I also said, 'Una, can't you learn to play something else other than that baguette by Earwig?' You were indignant. You reminded me it was a bagatelle, and that it was disrespectful of me to call a genius like Ludwig van Beethoven, Earwig."

"Beethoven was almost deaf when he wrote 'Für Elise'. You forgot that, Roland." My mother starts to sob. Has she suddenly remembered that Roland, seven years older than her, died in a motorcycle accident when she was eleven? An unspoken-about tragedy in her family – the loss of what had been and what would never be. It had broken her parents' marriage; her father guilty in his grief for he had loaned Roland the money for the bike, and her mother unforgiving in her pain because he had done so despite her misgivings. My mother? Never one to flee from life, she chose to embrace its beauty alongside the terrifying and the unknowable.

She always played 'Für Elise' to commemorate Roland's birthday, each yearly rendition imbued with the intellectual challenge and improvisational flair of a new arrangement, so she wouldn't vex him in his afterlife as she had sometimes done in this. But there was, in all the pieces my mother liked to play, a melancholy, a longing that existed alongside the brightness-of-being within her.

In all of ten seconds her mind switches to birthdays, the fragment of connection to Roland gone. "Do you think my husband will be coming soon ... it's my birthday, and I want to dance?" I hear her laugh and imagine her hands flowing in beautiful shapes as they always did when she was excited.

"He will. We better get you ready."

"Am I a nuisance?"

"No, *never*. You're a sweetheart. Let's find you a pretty dress, do your hair and make-up, and you'll be like Cinderella at the ball."

"*No* ... go away! *I'm not Cinderella.* I want to stay at home. *Leave me alone!*"

How my father stays so calm. "I'm sorry I upset you, Una. I was trying to help."

He must carry such a heavy burden inside. When he used to speak to me on the phone, he always seemed oblivious to the magnitude of his ability to care.

"No one's going to take you away. Here will always be your home. Close your eyes, Una, and listen. What do you hear inside the room?"

"The grandfather clock."

"Yes. It's tick-tock and chimes will always remind you of where you are ... at home. For everything else, I will always be there to remember for you."

"You are a good man. You're just like my husband."

"I am your husband, Una."

"Yes, you are, and you love me."

"We love one another very much."

I press the stop button on the recorder and put it down. Where did he learn his techniques to meet my mother's physical and emotional needs? Simple. He was a deeply loving man. That's all he needed to be able to validate, acknowledge and empathise. I'm face to face with the fact that there's a hardness in me that was neither in my mother nor is in my father. Is it a lack of patience or a throwback to a paternal family flaw?

I go to the kitchen and pour a Merlot into a large bulbous long-stemmed glass. I need to think about what is recorded and what is not and the gap between the two. The velvet-red of the wine caresses my mouth and suffuses my body with the fullness of black cherry and plum and the smoothness of Lindt dark chocolate balls. My body and mind mellow and calm. Slowly it comes to me … to protect my mother my father entered her reality. He knew not to torture her with the impossible task of travelling into his world. To protect me he altered reality for the self-same reason. It seemed like control at the time, almost exclusion – my stuff getting in the way again. He ensured that the times I saw and spoke to my mother were those when she was having a clearer day. He'd wait till my mother was back from the wasteland to the land of her smiling. The Land of 'Yes' and 'No' and 'Hi, sweetie'.

As her Alzheimer's progressed, and I rang from my new overseas placement in London, my father would say, "I won't disturb her now, Kate. Listen, she's about to play Chopin's 'Prelude in E Minor'. I'll leave the phone off the hook so you can listen. Just hang up when she's finished."

Such a simple haunting piece of light and dark that I know so well. My mother's favourite.

I top up my wine and begin the recording from where it left off. It's as if the unit has channelled my thoughts – Chopin's 'Prelude in E'. The first *b* saddens the *c* that follows. Reflective and tragic, it is a piece that goes from a place far away, to home. I close my eyes and listen. I see her right-hand curve, slow and elegant as a swan's neck as it strokes the keys of the Steinway baby grand. Her left relaxed as it caresses three notes, to the right's one. Gifted, she held all the music in her head. I cry as the music reaches its powerful climax and then, like me, moves away as if exhausted by emotion.

I didn't know it at the time, but it's becoming clear my father would be strategic with the days he rang me.

"Hello, baby girl, thought I'd ring for a quick catch-up while your mother's having her breakfast. She's having her favourite smoothie: banana, kefir yoghurt, spinach, blueberries, freshly ground linseed and one of Henrietta's eggs. Say hello to Kate, darling." With this prompt and a newly acquired effusiveness, my mother always said, "Hi, sweetie." It covered all bases.

"Father?"

"Yes."

"You must be exhausted. I'm thinking of ..."

"No need, Kate ... *Really* ... I'm coping fine."

The smoothie? Well, I realise now, she couldn't swallow well anymore. I'm sure she protested at the toddler sippy cup. I know my father – he blended enough for two.

The tacked-together fragments of the fabric of her memory, unravelling patchwork connections of decaying threads. My father shouldered all this in loving silence as his beloved unfixable wife disappeared before his eyes, and he before hers, with appalling irreversibility.

Why did my father not submit this tape in his defence? Atonement for his actions? Disdain for mercy-tempered justice? When he chose to end her suffering, she was already too late for death with dignity, an easy death, a good death. Outsource, isolate, sedate? Abandon her to the anonymity and loneliness of a white cotton gown, a single room and a steel entry door that, as it secured, also imprisoned? He could not do it. She did not want it. She was sixty-one and, after eight years, he did not shirk what she had asked of him. He curtailed the vandal that pillaged and plundered from my mother the compass of place and time, autonomy of reasoning and judgment, the memory of loved ones and music itself. He did it in the time of the 'befores'.

Before she deteriorated into a vacated carapace. Unknowing. Unmoving. Unspeaking.

Before it strangled the automatic ease of breath itself.

Before complete invisibility.

My father released her knowing that Death with insidious ferocity had already come for my mother five years ago. It had come in time-lapse, lingered and placed her in a holding bay.

The jury's verdict was unduly harsh – a testimony to assumption. Smothering registered, along with my father's waxwork figure, shadowed eyes and hidden fault lines of grief, as too callous, too brutal. The last part of the tape tells it was not so. I hear 'Au Clair de la Lune' in the background.

"I cradle you dead. The colour of it is like your greying hair, the lack of animation, the cold …" He breaks down as fathomless, mournful sobs engulf him. In control of himself, he continues, "You opened your eyes for a flicker. I so needed to believe I saw a thank you in them. Your breath light, slow and sickly sweet. I held you in my arms, pressed against the pillow and my chest. The moonlight cradled us both. A light for lovers. A light for those who need to find their way in the dark. A light to follow into the river of illumination and warmth that is home. You will always be home to me, Una. Remember me to everyone, my darling."

I know what I must do.

When I visit my father in prison, it is one of those quiet days when the spring rain falls sweetly warm and the damp soil is redolent of new beginnings, of seeds stirring in the nourishing darkness pushing knowingly upward into the air and light. I am shocked when I see him. He is stooped and the timbre of his voice hoarse. I try to keep my thoughts from showing on my face. He keeps his hands beyond my sight, but when I hand him the Intention to Appeal I see the tremor in his left hand like an indecisive dragonfly. "With the evidence of the recordings, there are compelling grounds for an appeal to challenge the conviction. You just need to sign this." I see the look on his face. "Don't worry. It'll be a private affair. The Court of Criminal Appeal is a closed court; only three judges form the panel, and the majority view prevails. I've hired one of Australia's leading silks, Terry Winston, from Sir Owen Dixon Chambers. He's confident the conviction will be squashed, and you'll be acquitted on the spot. No need for a retrial."

"How confident, Kate?"

"I'd be betting my redundancy money on it, and that's a six-figure sum. In Terry's words, 'They'll decide it's not in the public interest when you were motivated wholly by love and compassion and your wife's wishes.' Basically, the original conviction will be considered unduly severe and oppressive in light of the new evidence."

He's hesitating. He diverts. "Redundant?"

"Yes, voluntary redundancy. Time to be there for you as you were for Mother. You have a shed full of furniture that needs restoring. I have a soft enticing sales pitch and killer business acumen. Sign on the dotted line. What do you say?"

"You're sure about this, Kate?"

"Do I have a Montblanc pen, or what?"

He takes it and signs. *Yes!*

I hug him and say, "Father, I need you. I love you. I'm so sorry for what I didn't do."

As I embrace him, I can feel he has nothing more to give – I am hugging a husk. Now, it is time for me to banish the shadow of my paternal grandfather that follows me. My penance will be the soft voice, the steady hands and the heart that serves. For that, I am grateful.

⟨⟩ FOOTLOOSE AND FOOTSORE

I have spread my dreams under your feet

Tread softly because you tread on my dreams.

William Butler Yeats

When did my addiction commence? Dependencies are commonly a slide into enslavement. Mine was not. I stepped into it. However, common to all addictions its roots were in my childhood – the place that provides the groundwork for the rest of our lives.

Although my hair is grey, I still savour the catalyst for my shoe addiction – a pair of shiny black patent leather 'Mary Janes' with a buttoned ankle-strap. I was ten. Oh, how I reminisce about those shoes that encased both my feet and my heart. I adored them. When my mother threw them out, soles cratered with holes, I retrieved them from the bin. It was my first lesson in love – it is letting go. My Mary Janes were beyond salvage. What captivated and drew me? It was their glamour and beauty and their blatant shine that outshone all others. No commonplace child's shoe, they had no buckles or laces. Their buttonhole and button fastening hinted of a bygone era, of the unique and, as they belonged to *me*, I *was* the chosen child.

Shoes enchant with their newness. Too well-worn, scuffed and creased and their talismanic quality is lost – wonder, rapture and promise vanished.

Shoes are like lovers. The first exquisite pair always lingers, and all the later ones either remind us of how far we've come or what was lost never to be felt in the same way again. Each pair of shoes is a love affair. I am seduced by the curve of a heel, the elegant line of a toe, the extravagance of embellishment and the intoxicating use of colour. I'm impressed by attention to detail, innovative design and how a shoe complements my foot. I melt under the caress of buttery leather or the frippery of fabric knowing, even before I peruse the price tag, what has seduced my eyes and imprisoned my heart will be a costly liaison. Too late, the chemistry is instant and my debit card is in my outstretched hand. There is no reasoning when one is head over heels.

What marks me as an addict?

For starters, comfort never comes before style nor practicality before beauty. There is also the belief that no number of shoes is adequate. Walking on my way to the bank, an appointment, the supermarket, even driving, if there is a shoe shop it lures me like siren song. Addiction is owning eight pairs of black shoes when certainly two pairs would do. It's the handyman building multiple shelves in your walk-in wardrobe to house them and then, seeing them all amassed in one spot, knowing you would be embarrassed to invite your friends to marvel at his handiwork.

When it comes to shoes, one thing I've never understood is why Cinderella lost her glass slipper at the ball (apart from the fact it was vital to the storyline). Come on, girl, we all know it's possible to do the impossible in the highest of heels. In my prime I've danced in the highest of stilettos supremely and impossibly foot sure, kicked up my heels, even taken to my heels – all without keeling over or leaving a shoe behind. I've been 'head over heels' in love in my time but while I certainly believe most men are not heels, I've reached that stage in life when I certainly wouldn't lose a shoe over one.

When it comes to choosing shoes to complete an outfit, I've never had 'both feet on the ground'. Shoes – the ultimate accessory. Elegance and style always win out on practicality unless I'm going for a bushwalk. It's the one place I put function over fashion for fear of ridicule and a broken ankle.

What no one ever mentions, especially dieting gurus, is the proven fact that a twelve centimetres heel is an automatic way to look two-and-a-half kilos thinner. No dieting, no liposuction. Why are women not told this? When you factor in the cost of cosmetic procedures, those designer Italian leather shoes are a real bargain.

Despite fashion trends, nothing surpasses the sophisticated seductiveness and the finely tapered femininity of a well-proportioned stiletto and the lyrically elegant shoes created by Roger Vivier in the sixties, seventies and eighties. I feel the allure of a peep-toe, a slip-on, even a wedge but *never* sneakers, carpet slippers or crepe-soles. They are *objet sans d'art*.

Yes, shoes please the eye and flatter the foot, but they are so much more – they possess the magic of fairy tales. A pair of shoes transforms and transposes us from the humdrum and humble to Cinderella at the ball. You'll outrun your troubles in sneakers, but the only real means of escape from the ordinary is in the stiletto. Such a shoe transports us from the world of the fur slipper, *en vair*, to the world of glamour and grace that is the glass slipper, *en verre*.

I cherish shoes, but long ago something changed. Not an epiphany but a gradual inner need to scale things back, to simplify. I rediscovered where I was meant to be after my Mary Janes had led me astray all those years ago. I rediscovered 'barefoot on the beach'. My feet are no longer primarily carriers for those icons of style and status but are a vital channel of communication between myself and Mother Earth. Contours, arches, heels and toes connect with nature's life-affirming vibrations. Energy not enervation. Soothed not sored.

By surrendering to the natural sensuality of bare feet on sand and in saltwater, I found freedom from the artifice of sexuality that is the shoe upon the foot. Even then, adornment and elegance linger. My toenails are manicured, my Kundalini Hustle nail polish immaculate and my heels smooth and uncracked. I've discarded my shoes, yes, but I still love those feet of mine.

Although well-shod, no matter how many paths I'd travelled in my stilettos, I discovered my path to oneness with the world was barefoot. I asked myself, *If I had no beautiful shoes, would I feel stripped*

bare of my identity in the world? Am I willing to meet myself, and others,
barefoot or down-at-heel?

Letting go is the path to freedom – shoes are no longer a bunch
of flowers I must buy. They are the flowers growing wild whose
beauty pleasures me but no longer urges me to ownership. I've
swapped 'sole' for 'soul'. My need to own shoes was merely a ploy to
distract or perhaps, as some theories declare, a symbolic search for
enlightenment.

Footnotes for the addict:

- Do not feel guilty about the number of shoes you own. It is a well-known
  fact, from the Middle Ages to the present day, women buy more
  shoes than men.
- Spare no expense for the luxury and glamour of the perfect shoe.
- Clothes maketh the man and shoe the woman.
- Never ask a woman, unless she's a close friend, where she bought her
  divine pair of shoes. She's sure to lie or be evasive.
- Never let shoes languish. Organise purpose-built shelving and admire
  your brood daily.
- Shoes are sculptures for the feet. You are a Patron of the Arts.
- Be well-heeled always.
- All hail Dior, Roger Vivier and the fifties for creating the first authentic
  stiletto and doing great things for women's butts and bosoms.
- Only cut your fingernails on a Thursday, as superstition says this is sure
  to bring more shoes.
- Walking in high heels is as efficacious for the lower body as a workout at
  the gym. It expends two-and-a-half times more energy than walking on
  lower heels, as it counters the forward thrust of the body.

Footnotes for the reformed addict:

- An exquisite pair of Italian leather shoes offers beauty, glamour and
  elegance, but it's friends with their authenticity, humour and constancy
  who make a real difference in life. Besides, a haute-couture shoe has no
  tongue and is never going to tell you when food remnants grout your teeth.

- Never judge anyone unless you've walked five hundred metres in their shoes. After that, who cares? You're out of sight, and you've acquired a new pair of shoes – hopefully, Jimmy Choos.
- Replace wisdom for wedges, power for pumps, strength for stilettos, empathy for espadrilles, soul for sole and inner-healing for well-heeled. Why? These necessary qualities support you through everything life throws your way.
- It's okay to own those gorgeous red stilettos if you also own a set of screwdrivers and a cordless drill.
- If you decide to learn Spanish as a foreign language, show how far you've come since your addiction by not quitting the class as soon as you've learnt to ask, "*Donde Dolce and Gabbana?*"

Well, my addiction aired and shared, it's time for my Wednesday yoga class, and it'll take me at least twenty minutes to totter there in my stilettoes, but oh, the bliss when I arrive, take them off, and my bare feet kiss the mat.

✐ F**K LOVE

FUCK LOVE! Ripped away in a moment.

Would he have loved me if he wasn't a dead-man-waiting?

Would he have wanted more perfection, more of the exceptional both physically and intellectually?

Would his lust have led him astray someplace along the line if time didn't dictate he had one relationship left to end his days?

I feel like the cup on a shelf in a reject shop. An imperfect bargain for a shopper with limited resources. I want to scream, "*Fuck you!*" Not feel pissy, silent tears trickle over my soft cheeks.

I want to roar, "*You're like all the fucking rest!*" Yet he's done nothing but love me.

As we lay in bed, he holds me and I weep, silent and still. I look into his eyes and see the coolness of old betrayals. I see another's eyes, cold, shark-like. Even his facial contours become the 'Other'. Humiliation. Rejection. Man-slut!

I tell it silently ... fuck off.

The face morphs back into the present and he who holds me.

Why the hell am I unable to relax into trusting? Love between man and woman is like the weather, constant but capricious. The past floods me. I relive the betrayals. The slice of cold steel slashing my heart and lungs, leaving me flaying like a speared fish, asphyxiated. Air without water is not oxygen. Gutted. Thrown aside. No second glances. It is the other woman who has triggered all this – the one with the pussy one cock is unable to fill. The woman at the drinks and hors d'oeuvres social we attend on the final night of the three-day writing course.

I've read, all betrayal requires is opportunity and need. She has something he values. He admires the way she writes and her expertise. I do too. From the few short excerpts I read in an anthology, she has a hard-hitting style. Raw. No holds barred. During the conversation she told him he'd have no trouble with the publication of an autobiography. She'd be happy to read whatever he wrote and proffer her opinion. FOC – Free of Charge. Fuck Of Course.

I do not trust a woman who says 'wank' and 'fuck' in a conversation and then adds, "I shouldn't say that, should I?" with a touch of his arm. In your face with the coy. *Please!* A woman who writes, 'She straddled the dying campfire and pissed slowly. She wanted him to watch her.' I want to hang a sign – Trespassers Keep Out. She's not his type physically or emotionally, but few men desist when offered a sure thing.

She's a woman who, talking to us as a couple, is all focus on him. I barely receive a sideward glance nor does the man with her. Her strategy fails. I am no outsider. I regret my openness with her and the personal snippets she gleaned from our conversation. She seemed surprised we had only been together a year.

They continue to chat about the writing course and its focus on courage. From out of the blue, he comes out with, "Olinda is courageous." It catches me by surprise. From her, a split moment of silence and a look. She does not want to be complicit in singing my praises. I'm the enemy.

Such a woman says 'fuck' to the usual moral boundaries. She'd fuck another woman's man. I'm not sure she would do this. Neither is she ... *yet*. She's strident, would be demanding, highly sexed. She has a certain softness, but a harshness overlays it. She has the persona of an abused woman. Women who swing between nurturing mother and destructive vamp. Hard to live with in the long term. She'd call a spade a spade. Spit in your face. Hurl harsh words. Then again, perhaps it's the other woman who is more of a threat. The lonely one who earlier engaged us both in conversation, drink in one hand and hors d'oeuvre in the other, compliant and not at all in your face.

Fuck love!

He leaves and wanders in the direction of the bar for drinks. The FOC woman invites me over to meet the man with her. A nice enough man. Why hasn't she eaten him for dinner yet? Perhaps she has cancer too. They don't go together. He's certainly not a choice she'd have made in her younger days. She attributes the wrong name to me. Not an intentional slight. I don't take it as such. Merely a lack of interest and focus. She asks me a couple of questions without animation and, when the drinks return, I leave the three of them to converse. I mingle. I angle past two men who smile and say hello. One has a striking pink shirt with floral motifs. He carries it with style and confidence.

"Good evening to the two of you. I'm Olinda."

I turn to the one in the floral and pink, "I love your shirt. Tell me its story."

Our conversation is fun. There's laughter. I sparkle. *Up yours,* I think, forgetting predatory women drool over a trophy even more if it's stolen from a woman whose company other men enjoy.

Back at the hotel I am unable to share any of this with him. He sits and writes across from me at the glass dining table. The metre of transparency between us is a sheet of thin ice. Proceed at your own risk. I'm falling through. Vertical thrashing. I haven't the attire to stay afloat, to keep my head above water. He has no idea of the angst across from him. If I share it, I fear he'll think me insecure. He will think I am weak and unfillable. I do not trust there will be compassion. He continues to write. I settle, turn around to thicker ice, mind-pick myself to the solid horizontal and roll back to standing safety and equilibrium.

I am a fool to worry about another woman when the brazen slut he will close his eyes to, sweat and stiffen to, who'll numb him to me, will be Death herself. A hard-hearted whore eager only for breath and tears. *This* is the forever loss to fear.

Alina Loneck was born in Nottingham in the UK in 1953 and has lived in Australia since 1976. She has an Honours Degree in Psychology and English Literature from Leeds University and a Bachelor of Visual Arts from Sydney College of the Arts.

Although an educator and artist, her most precious roles in life have been as mother and friend.

This is her second collection of short stories. Her first novella 'Searching for North' was included in her first collection *Within Sunshine & Shadow*. She is currently working on her second novella, a love story about the joys and challenges of a mature-aged romance.

Also, by Alina Loneck

Non-Fiction

Opals, Rivers of Illusions, Gemcraft Publications,
Index ISBN 978-0-9092232-4-3

Fiction

Within Sunshine and Shadow, Cilento Publishing,
Index ISBN 978-0-6450004-4-3
(Three short stories and a novella)

MY THANKS AND ACKNOWLEDGMENTS

My deepest thanks to my two beta readers who gave me feedback from a reader's point of view. Helen Lambert, dear friend and kindred spirit, your reading of my manuscript twice showed the dedication and support of a true friend. Thank you also for being a sounding board for the order in which the stories are presented; you have a keen sensibility for authenticity and the reader's emotional journey. Rachel Faith, fellow writer and valued friend, I thank you for your generosity of spirit in sharing with me that you thought I had arrived as a writer. I thank you too for your astute honesty in pointing out I hadn't quite got there with my original draft of 'The Tattooed Sorceress'. Here's to the debut novel you are working on. May I, and the world, have it in the palms of our hands soon.

My joyous thanks to Sandra Wood who is friend, artist and alchemist. Your artworks for the cover (front and back) are stunning visual metaphors for the stories in the collection. As delightfully modest as you are, the world needs to know you have an incredible eye for form, composition and colour and that you are adept with an impressive array of mediums.

My acknowledgement and thanks to the developmental editor Helen Williams who assessed my pre-final draft. You pinpointed the strengths in my writing: psychological precision, ability for drama but also nuance, the courage to get down and dirty with the hard truths and to amuse and offer insight.

My deep gratitude to Evan Shapiro of Green Avenue Design and Cilento Publishing for the expertly formatted layout for the cover and the internals of the book. As a collection of forty-seven stories of varied length and format, the layout was not a straightforward exercise, but throughout it all you were always patient, personable, knowledgeable and generous with your time and expert guidance. I trusted my book in your hands from the very start. You're a five-star Google review.

To my darling friend Jennifer McAleer, whether in rose petal times or thorn, your friendship and enthusiastic support is a treasured constant.

Finally, a deeply loving acknowledgement to my two adult children, Alex and Natka. Loving you, and being loved in return, is a many splendored thing.

www.ingramcontent.com/pod-product-compliance
Lightning Source LLC
Chambersburg PA
CBHW070612120726
47909CB00004B/1183